MY

Please return/renew this item
by the last date shown.
Books may also be renewed by
phone and Internet
Telford and Wrekin Libraries

THE BERLIN SPY TRAP

John Stack awakes to find himself in a hotel bedroom in Spain, with a partial loss of memory. He knows that he is working for British Intelligence, and that Berak is dead and Gunter has taken over. He has to get to Berlin as quickly as possible and fill the missing gaps in his memory. But the opposition is still looking for him. He goes to the Doctor who offers him help if he will negotiate the escape of an East German across the Wall. Stack agrees, and returns to Berlin with the girl, to find that his two missions are closely linked together.

THE BERLIN SPY TRAP

THE BERLIN SPY TRAP

by

Geoffrey Davison

Magna Large Print Books
Long Preston, North Yorkshire,
BD23 4ND, England.

British Library Cataloguing in Publication Data.

Davison, Geoffrey
    The Berlin spy trap.

    A catalogue record of this book is
    available from the British Library

    ISBN   978-0-7505-3667-7

First published in Great Britain in 1974 by Robert Hale & Co.

Copyright © Geoffrey Davison 1974

Cover illustration © Collaboration JS by arrangement with
Arcangel Images

The moral right of the author has been asserted

Published in Large Print 2013 by arrangement with
Geoffrey Davison, care of Watson, Little Ltd.

Magna Large Print is an imprint of Library Magna Books Ltd.

Printed and bound in Great Britain by
T.J. (International) Ltd., Cornwall, PL28 8RW

1

As he awoke, he felt the pool of perspiration around his body and a dull ache at the back of his head. He partially opened his eyes and vaguely saw a dirty, yellow ceiling. He closed his eyes again. Where was he, he wondered drowsily? Where was he? He got no answer. He shuffled about in the bed and wished that his head would stop aching. Where was he? The question registered in his brain, but again got no answer. He felt a moment of panic. Where was he? He opened his eyes fully. They stared at the yellow ceiling and focused on a series of cracks. He lay quite still, staring at the ceiling. His head ached, and he also felt a numbness in the pit of his stomach. It was a strange feeling. One that he hadn't experienced before.

'Where am I?' he mumbled. 'Where am I?'

His voice sounded deep and strange. He became agitated. He sat upright. The room looked unfamiliar. It was a hotel bedroom, he thought. He saw a notice on the wall, above an old chest of drawers, and another on the bedroom door. There was a half-opened, green-louvred shutter at the window, through which a blaze of sunlight stabbed across the room. He turned his head, and saw a wash-basin and a wardrobe that matched the chest of drawers in age and appearance. The walls of the room were a dirty yellow, like the ceiling. The floor was bare linoleum – colour brown.

He flopped back on the bed and groaned. Where was he? His hand went to the back of his head and touched congealed blood. He also felt blood on his temple. Again he groaned.

'How did I get here?' he asked aloud.

He closed his eyes and tried to remember, but his memory was like a sponge. It yielded nothing. Who am I, he asked himself? There was a delay. Panic seized him. Who was he? Perspiration came to his brow. His brain responded, and he sighed with relief. He lay quite still. He knew who he was, but he also knew that he had a problem. He was John Stack, a foreign correspondent, but he was also working for British Intelligence! He was working for British Intelligence and he didn't know where he was! He swallowed hard. Collect your thoughts together quickly, he told himself. Get all the facts. Go back over the ground. Be systematic; sort it out. Your name is John Stack, you are thirty-five years of age. You worked in Fleet Street and then joined the European Press Agency in Berlin. Berlin! Yes, he thought, he knew Berlin well. Berlin meant Max Schafer, his editor in chief. It also meant Sue. He screwed his eyes into their sockets. Sue! He felt a barrier automatically clamp down inside of him. She hadn't understood, he thought. She hadn't even tried. But then, how could she? He had never told her anything. He had never been allowed to. His recall to London, and his meeting with that cold fish from MI6, had all to be kept a secret. No one was to know. He had been conscripted into MI6 and given an assignment, but he couldn't talk about it, not even to his wife. So Sue had eventually walked out on him. Yes, he thought, he remembered Berlin all right. And he also remembered Prague. Prague was where it had all begun, and Prague meant Berak. The dull ache in the pit of his stomach became stronger. He remembered Prague and he remembered Berak. Berak had been a journalist like Stack. He had also been sympathetic towards the West, so British Intelligence had wanted someone to cultivate him. That someone had been Stack. His assignment had been to build up a cell around Berak and push them to their limit, and then further. He was remembering fast. There had been another journalist whom he had also tried to recruit – Karl Gunter from East Germany. The three had met in Stack's bedroom as the Russian tanks had patrolled the streets. Berak had agreed to come into Stack's cell. Gunter had held back. He was sympathetic, but without contacts, and he was returning to Berlin. Berak was the man with the links and the urgency. Stack could feel the tension of those meetings vividly, almost as if it was yesterday. But it wasn't yesterday, he thought, not yesterday. It was a lifetime ago. There had been so many secret meetings. Meetings in the spring, in the summer, and in the winter. Meetings in parks, in cafés, in hotels. It had been a long time ago when it had all begun. A long, long time ago. He had travelled back and forward over the years between Berlin and Prague, but Sue hadn't understood why, and he had become too committed to pull out. Too committed and too involved. It had become part of him. He couldn't pull out, so he had continued with his meetings and Sue had walked out on him. He remembered his last meeting with Berak in Czechoslovakia had been in the December. They had met in a wood outside Prague. It had been bitterly cold; there had been snow on the ground. Berak had told him that he was being sent to East Berlin. Stack had been pleased, very pleased. So had his Control. Berlin was Stack's base, his own backyard. It would be easier for them to operate there. So Control had arranged for Stack to follow Berak to Berlin.

Stack stared at the bedroom wall ahead of him. He had returned to Berlin in the December – last December. Go on, he told

10

himself. Go on! Berlin!

In Berlin they had continued with their operation, he thought. Berak still had his contacts, and he had made others. But in Berlin it hadn't been the same. There had been failures and arrests. Something had gone sour. Berak had wanted to get out. Stack closed his eyes as he remembered. Berak had wanted to get out, but Stack wouldn't let him leave. Something big was in the pipeline. Something very big. Berak had to remain until someone could take over. They had gone back to Gunter – Karl Gunter. Gunter had been hesitant, but he had finally been persuaded. Gunter had been persuaded to take over from Berak, and Berak had wanted help to flee to the West. What next, Stack asked himself? What had happened after that? He got no answer. Go on, he thought desperately, remember! Go on, damn you, remember!... But his mind was like cotton wool. It had absorbed all the fluid of past memories that it was going to take. It wouldn't respond. There was a barrier where Gunter had agreed to take over and Berak had wanted to get out.

And now where was he, Stack wondered? Where the hell was he?

He slid out of bed and stood up. His head throbbed as if he had an almighty hangover. He staggered across the room to a mirror above the washbasin and looked at his face.

It looked as if it had been roughened up a bit and seen life, but it was familiar. Thank God for that, he thought. At least it was familiar. He looked at it again. It was tanned, blue-eyed and determined. He saw the thick, jet black hair, the dark eyebrows, the determined chin with its dark stubble, and the colourful bruise to his temple. He bared his teeth. They were reasonably well cared for and they were his own. He grimaced at the mirror and ran his hand through his hair. His fingers touched the bruise at the back of his head and he winced. He examined it in the mirror, but it was covered with congealed blood and hair. How had he got that, he wondered? Who had hit him?

'Where am I?' he asked himself aloud. There was more aggression in his voice. If only his head would stop aching, he thought. 'Take it easy,' he mumbled. 'It will come. Just take it easy.'

He doused himself with cold water and dried himself on a towel. He caught sight of the notice of the wall and his heart sank. Hotel San Miguel, it read. Gerona Province. My God, he thought! Spain! He was in Spain! He swallowed hard and got a grip of himself. If he was in Spain there would be a reason. Take it easy, he kept saying to himself. It will come back to you.

He went over to the window and opened the shutters. Spread out before him was a panoramic view of the mountainside reaching down to the plain. Intermingling with the ochre, green and brown vegetation were orange roofs and off-white buildings. In the distance was a blue haze. He must be in the mountains, he thought, probably not far from Barcelona. Why, he asked himself? Why? He got no answer. He looked up at the sky. It was a clear blue, and the sun was shining, but it didn't help. He closed the shutters. Instinctively he felt there was a need for secrecy. He knew that he had to be careful. He tried to shake off the feeling, but it persisted. Suddenly he wanted to get out of the room. Away from the hotel. Panic gripped him. He perspired, and then felt quite calm again.

He looked around for his clothes and found them in the wardrobe. He felt in the pockets for his wallet. It wasn't there. He became agitated again. Where the hell was his wallet? And his passport? He went to the bed and lifted the pillow. He saw his wallet and passport, and felt much easier. He picked up his passport and examined it. On the front it had, 'Mr J Stack'. Inside he read, Name of bearer: Mr John Stack. He turned to the second page and saw his photograph. It wasn't a good likeness. He read some of the particulars. Profession: Foreign Correspondent. Country of Residence: England. Height: six feet and half an inch. Colour of eyes: Blue. Colour of hair: Black. Special Peculiarities: None. He examined the other pages. He could have been a travel courier. It was marked on almost every page. He had travelled Europe on both sides of the Iron Curtain. He put it to one side. What was he doing in Spain, he wondered? Was it an assignment for E.P.A.? He got no answer and he silently cursed. How long was he going to have this blankness, he asked himself? How long? Something was imminent. He felt it. There was an urgency. He had to recover his memory. He just had to. He moved the pillow to one side to collect his wallet and saw a silver cigarette case. He picked it up. His initials were on the case. There were five cigarettes inside. He put one to his mouth, but his stomach reacted to the suggestion of smoke. He put the cigarette back in the case. He emptied the contents of his wallet on to the bed. There were some Spanish and German notes; a book of Eurocheques; a carbon copy of a Lufthansa flight ticket and three cards. He looked at the flight ticket. It was for a first-class single flight from Berlin to Barcelona dated June 30th, arrival time in Barcelona 16.00 hours. He glanced at his watch. It gave the date as July 2nd. Nine-fifteen on July 2nd. He had been in Spain less than forty-eight hours, he thought. But why Barcelona, he wondered? He picked up the cheque book. The

14

instructions were printed in German. He read them without effort. He read them out aloud. He could speak and understand German fluently, he thought. At least he hadn't forgotten that. He looked at the three cards. One showed his photograph and identified him as a representative of the European Press Agency in Berlin. Another gave the E.P.A. office address in Berlin, together with Stack's name and the name of the Berlin chief editor, Max Schafer.

'Max Schafer,' he said aloud. Yes, he thought, he remembered Max Shafer. He could even picture Shafer's rough, scraggy face, and see the ever-present cigar sticking out of Schafer's mouth. Yes, Schafer was familiar.

The third card gave a room number – No. 406, at the Hotel Excelsior, Avenida Generalissimo, Barcelona. It was dated June 30th.

There was also a letter addressed to Stack at the E.P.A. office in Berlin. The writing on the envelope was small and neat. The postmark was blurred, but the stamp was Czech. He withdrew the letter and read it. It was written in German and signed by Anna Berak. 'Dear Herr Stack,' it read, 'I am writing to let you know that we were officially notified, yesterday, that Emil was shot, dead, whilst trying to cross the border at Fenstadt, and has been buried there in the village. My mother and I wish to thank you

15

for all your kindness and help to Emil'.

Stack groaned. He felt as if a knife had pierced his stomach and was tearing at all his raw nerves. He remembered now. Gunter had taken over from Berak, but Stack had not been able to help Berak escape. Finally Berak had arranged his own escape, only to be shot, dead, in the attempt. Kindness and help! Stack's kindness had been to push Berak past the point of no return. His help had been to stand by and let him get himself killed. He gritted his teeth and looked at the letter again. There was no address on it to which he could reply, only the date, June 27th. He must have received it just before leaving Berlin, he thought. He clenched his fist. Berak! Gunter! They were all so close to him. Now Berak was dead. He closed his eyes and tried to bring himself up to date. Why was he in Spain? Why? The cotton wool gave nothing away. He cursed vocally.

A knock on his bedroom door made him start.

'Come in,' he called out in English.

The door opened and a youthful-looking waiter entered the room carrying a tray. He smiled at Stack, showing his white teeth.

'*Buenos dias,* Señor,' he said, placing the tray on the chest of drawers.

'*Buenos dias,*' Stack replied.

The waiter poured out a cup of coffee. Stack watched him.

'You speak English?' Stack asked. *'Inglés?'*

The waiter smiled. 'Leetle,' he said apologetically.

'When did I arrive?' Stack asked.

The waiter looked puzzled.

'One night?' Stack asked. He pointed to the bed. *'Uno noche?'* he asked.

'Sí, Señor,' the waiter replied eagerly. 'You a leetle...' He shook his head from side to side. *'Anoche.'*

Stack got the message. He had been in a bit of a daze when he had arrived the previous evening. He made an action of driving a car. 'Come by automobile?' he asked.

'Sí, Señor.'

'From Barcelona?' Stack asked.

The waiter shrugged. Stack repeated the question. The waiter shook his head.

'Aeroplano,' the waiter said, and spread out his arms like a flying aircraft. *'Aeroplano –* whoof!' he added.

'Air crash?' Stack asked.

'Sí, Señor, *sí,'* the waiter said happily. *'Aeroplano* crash.'

Air crash! Stack's hand went to the back of his head. Had he been in an air crash, he wondered? No, he thought. No. It wasn't possible. He had come by car. But there had been an air crash in the mountains, and he had come to the hotel from the scene of the air crash.

The waiter stood his ground. Stack took

out a note and gave it to him. The waiter's face lit up.

'*Gracias,* Señor,' he said.

Stack made a gesture to indicate that the waiter could leave.

'I no tell,' the waiter said, standing his ground.

'No tell who?' Stack asked.

Again the waiter looked puzzled. He held up his hand to display two fingers.

'*Dos hombres,*' he said. '*Anoche.*'

Two men last night! Two men had been looking for him, Stack thought. Two men he hadn't wanted to see. Who had they been? What had they wanted? He didn't like it. The feeling of urgency gripped him again. He had to get away. He gave the waiter another note and ushered him out of the room. Hurriedly he drank his coffee. He collected his belongings together. There wasn't much, but there was a small camera. He fingered it thoughtfully. It was loaded and set for action, but it hadn't been used. He replaced it in his grip bag and examined his suit. It was soiled and marked. He glanced at his hands. His knuckles were cut and chafed. He had been in a fight, he thought, and by all the signs it had been a grim battle. He got dressed. In his suit pocket, he found two sets of keys. One of them had a label attached to it giving the name of a garage in Barcelona. The other had no identity. He had hired a car to visit the air crash, he thought quickly. Air crash! Had he flown from Berlin to cover the air crash? Was that what he was doing in Spain?

He left the bedroom and walked cautiously along a narrow landing, and down a curved flight of stairs into the entrance hall. The hotel had a pleasant, simple, country, Spanish style about it, which Stack barely noticed. He had other things on his mind, and he was in a hurry. He settled his account and got the young waiter to take him to his car. It was a white Mercedes. The waiter returned to the hotel, and Stack examined the car. When he was satisfied that it was not booby trapped, he got in and drove out of the hotel grounds. He passed through a small village of dirty, yellow buildings, and on to a narrow, twisting road which meandered its way down the mountainside. He drove slowly, trying to relax himself and his thoughts, so that in the vacuum would come some of his missing past. He found he was surprisingly calm. He had come to Spain on an assignment. It had probably been for E.P.A., but his present physical condition suggested that he was still wearing two hats. And it had something to do with the air crash. Who had been on that plane, he wondered? He had to know.

The blast from a car horn interrupted his thoughts. He pulled to the side of the road as a white police car raced past him going up the mountain. Inside the police car were two uniformed policemen and two plain-clothed detectives. He watched them disappear out of view with mounting concern. He had a strong feeling that their arrival was somehow linked with his present condition. It was a feeling that he couldn't shake off as he continued his way down the mountain. He lost his calmness and developed an urgency to get away from the area. He was glad when he came to the main road to Barcelona and could increase his speed.

In Barcelona, he felt easier. The traffic was busy, and so were the boulevards and pavements. He returned the car to the garage and went by foot to the Avenida Del Generalissimo Franco. In the middle of the broad tree-lined roadway, white-helmeted police controlled the traffic. Stack's eyes flashed about him, searching for any danger. He passed a newspaper stand and saw two headlines which immediately coloured his thinking. The aeroplane that had crashed had been an Interflug aircraft, flying from Berlin Schonefeld Airport to Barcelona. An East German aircraft! Alongside the headlines of the air disaster was the news that the U.S. Vice-President and the American Sixth Fleet were arriving in Barcelona the following day.

He purchased several newspapers, both

British and German, and hurried to his hotel. The hotel foyer was cool and busy. He eyed the faces, suspiciously, as he crossed the marble paving. A man got up from a seat and walked towards the exit. He was of medium height and slim build, with flaxen hair. Stack watched him leave. He felt certain that they had met before, but he didn't know where. The man put on a pair of sunglasses and left the hotel.

Stack went up to the reception desk.

'I would like to settle my account,' he said. 'I am leaving.'

'Yes, Señor. Room number?'

Stack gave his room number.

'Ah, Señor Stack,' the receptionist commented, with more enthusiasm. 'There have been some telephone calls for you. Several from Berlin, and two from a Doctor Lorenzo.'

Berlin? That would be E.P.A., Stack thought, but he didn't know a Doctor Lorenzo. Or did he?

The receptionist produced the account. Stack paid by cheque and walked towards the lift.

'Señor Stack!' the receptionist called to him.

Stack stopped in his tracks and thought that everyone in the foyer had heard his name being called out. He turned to face the desk clerk again.

'Berlin are on the phone again,' the receptionist said apologetically.

Stack frowned visibly. He didn't want to speak to anyone, never mind Berlin. He dropped his head, lowered his eyes, and momentarily studied the marble mosaic on the floor. If he refused the call, he would attract attention to himself. He could feel people watching him. He had no alternative but to take it.

'In booth number two, Señor,' the receptionist smiled.

Stack went to the booth, and picked up the receiver.

'John?' a man's voice asked. It had a broad American accent. It was Max Schafer.

'Yes, Max,' Stack said.

'Say, what the hell has kept you? Where have you been?'

'In the mountains,' Stack replied guardedly.

'Sure, I know, but you were supposed to call me last night.'

Stack wondered what he should tell him.

'Where's the story?' Schafer asked.

'I don't have one,' Stack replied.

'What the hell sort of answer is that?'

Stack breathed heavily into the telephone.

'Say, are you okay?' Schafer asked.

'No,' Stack replied.

'What do you mean?'

'Something has happened.'

'Happened! What?'

22

'I don't know,' Stack replied. 'I've had an accident. My memory is a bit hazy.'

There was a momentary silence as the message sunk in.

'Your memory!' Schafer gasped. 'John, you aren't fooling me? This is Max you are speaking to.'

'That's okay, Max, I know you,' Stack said impatiently.

'Thank goodness for that,' Schafer sighed. 'What gives?'

'I seem to have forgotten some of the events over the past couple of weeks or so,' Stack said quietly. 'Even why, or how, I came to Spain.'

There was another silence as if Schafer was studying the problem. The small booth was becoming oppressive. It was airless. Stack's head began to throb.

'You flew to Spain to cover the American visit,' Schafer explained quickly, 'but give it a miss. The Madrid office are covering it as well. You need a doctor…'

'Sure,' Stack intervened. 'Look, when things sort themselves out…'

'John!' Schafer called to him anxiously. 'I want you back in Berlin as soon as possible.'

'Yeah!'

Stack rang off. Schafer was a ball of fire, but the way Stack was feeling, he cut no ice. There were more important things for Stack to attend to than Schafer's news agency in

Berlin. Such as getting his memory back for a start. He looked at himself in the small mirror above the telephone. The bruise on his temple was becoming more colourful, he thought. He also needed a shave. His eyes caught a man watching him from across the foyer. He was small, dark faced and white suited. Stack picked up his bag and looked in the mirror again. The man had gone – vanished. Stack shrugged. He was beginning to feel as if the whole world was against him.

He joined the queue for the lift. He missed out on the first shift, and it was a few minutes before he got to the fourth floor and room number 406. He opened the bedroom door, entered the room, and saw the dark-faced man who had been in the foyer, waiting for him. But it wasn't a welcome home reception. There was a sardonic smile on the man's dark face, and a small automatic pistol in his hand! Stack felt his inside freeze up and his face muscles go taut. In his present condition he wasn't going to be able to tell who was friend and who was foe. He took an instant dislike to his intruder, and the smirk on his face.

'Close the door, Señor Stack,' the man said gruffly, in English.

Stack closed the door. 'What do you want?' he growled, and walked into the room. It was a large, modern room, with the usual fittings and a separate bathroom. Stack took it all in as he walked purposely into the middle of the room. The man edged away.

'You know what I want,' the man replied. His eyes had narrowed. His face looked leaner and meaner. One hand went to a pocket and withdrew a fitment which he pointedly attached to his revolver, his eyes never leaving Stack.

'If you don't hand it over before I count five, Señor, I will shoot. I am not making an idle threat.'

Stack felt his mouth dry up. The man meant business.

'What is it you want?' he asked hastily.

'What you went up the mountains for,' the man hissed.

'The plane crash?' Stack asked.

'One... Two... Three...'

Stack's brains told him to act quickly, or he would be maimed by an expert gunman.

'Four...'

'Wait!' Stack called out desperately. 'I have it in my bag.'

He threw the bag on the floor, between himself and the gunman.

'Get it!' the man ordered. 'And no tricks.'

Stack bent down to the bag. The gunman was no expert, he thought, or he would have known the move. It made him feel happier. He had learned a few tricks over the years, and this was one of them. He got his feet in position, placed his two hands on the straps of the grip bag, and lunged with the bag at the gunman. As the bag collided with the white-suited figure, Stack was conscious of something passing perilously close to his face. There was a 'plop', and a clinking of falling glass, as the two men fell in a heap on the hard, tiled floor.

Furiously Stack's hand went for the gunman's wrist, but there was little resistance in the man. The fall had weakened him. Stack knocked the revolver to one side and lashed into the man's face. It became covered with blood. He grabbed the man's jacket and lifted him up from the floor.

'Who sent you?' he demanded angrily. 'Who sent you?' There was no response. He slapped the bloody face.

'Who sent you?' he shouted.

Again there was no response. He lashed out again, and felt the man's body go limp. He let go. The body sank to the floor. He looked down at it. It was a bloody mess. He picked up the man's hardware and put it in his bag. It might come in useful, he thought.

The body on the floor moved. Stack dragged it into the bathroom, and dumped it in the shower. He turned on the water. The body stirred, groaned and coughed. Stack dragged it out and left it in a heap outside the bathroom. When the man came to, he would question him again, he thought. He caught sight of his own hands. They were also a bloody red, and his head began to throb again. He went into the bathroom and turned on the taps of the washbasin. His knuckles were badly cut and bruised. There was also blood on his face. He washed it off, and wrapped the towel around his hands. The savagery of his blows appalled him. He had been like a killer. His throbbing head became a blinding pain. He screwed up his face and sat on the toilet seat. The pain gripped him. He buried his face in his hands. He heard a door being closed. It registered with him that either some reinforcements had come or the man had gone. He had to find out, and quick. He staggered into the bedroom. The figure on the floor had gone. The man hadn't been so near death as he had imagined. He opened the bedroom door and saw the gunman disappearing around the end of the corridor. He closed the door again. He felt too lousy to follow him. He stood quite still, leaning against the wall. Gradually the pain eased and became bearable. What the devil had the man been after, he wondered? What had he wanted? Was he one of the two men who had been asking for him at the hotel in the mountains? He slowly paced the floor. What was he supposed to have that the man wanted so badly? What? The camera hadn't been used and there was nothing else. What was it? He glanced at the wardrobe and cupboards. Perhaps there were some of his belongings in the bedroom that might help him to remember. He quickly examined the fittings, only to find that they were empty. He had been travelling surprisingly light.

The telephone started ringing. He looked at it hesitantly, then picked it up.

'Señor Stack?' the telephoonist asked.

'Yes,' Stack growled.

A call was switched through.

'Good morning, Señor Stack,' a man said in English.

Stack didn't recognise the voice, but its deep, bass tone suggested a man of large frame.

'My name is Lorenzo,' the man explained. 'Doctor Lorenzo. I tried to contact you yesterday – twice.'

'What about?' Stack asked suspiciously.

'I wanted to solicit your help,' Lorenzo said. His voice had a rich, cultural ring to it that commanded attention, and got it. 'However, I now feel we can be of mutual assistance to each other,' Lorenzo added.

'I don't follow you,' Stack said sharply.

'I suggest you come to my surgery where we can talk,' Lorenzo said. 'It is situated in a rather unpleasant district near the docks, but it suits my many interests. The address is No. 167 Calle Cadalla. I would also venture to suggest that you leave the hotel immediately, and discreetly.'

'Why?'

'I fear the police are about to pay you a visit. Goodbye, Señor Stack.'

Lorenzo rang off. Stack frowned and replaced the telephone on its stand. Who was this man Lorenzo, he wondered? How much notice should he take of his warning? He went to the balcony and got his answer. In the street below, he saw two uniformed policemen and a plain-clothed detective stepping out of a police car. They walked towards the hotel entrance. That was sufficient for him. They might not be coming for him, but he decided not to wait and find out. In his condition, he was no match for a verbal battle with the police. He grabbed his bag and newspapers and hurried down the secondary flight of stairs to the basement garage. Quickly he picked his way through the cars, up a ramp, and into the bright sunshine. He glanced about him. It was clear. He walked along the back street, checked that he wasn't being followed, and set out in a direction that would put the greatest distance between himself and the hotel. After about half an hour's walking, he found himself in an area of narrow alleyways, dirty, terraced buildings, and noisy traffic. He went to a small café, ordered a coffee, and studied the newspapers.

He looked at the British newspaper first.

He found a report on the air crash on the first page. An aircraft belonging to Interflug, the East German Airline, had crashed in the mountains, north of Barcelona. It had taken off from Berlin – Schonefeld Airport, on June 30th at 20.00 hours, with a party of East German journalists. He felt the dull ache inside of him again. The British newspaper gave no names, but he suspected the worst. He found the list of passengers in the German newspaper, and his heart sank. Karl Gunter's name was included. Karl Gunter had been on that aircraft after all! Sadly he put down the newspapers. Karl Gunter had been on that aircraft, and now Karl Gunter was dead. First Berak and now Gunter. He smacked his fist against his hand. Fate had played him another cruel blow. Gunter had been on his way to Barcelona, he thought. Had they arranged to meet? Had Gunter something important to pass? Was that why Stack had flown to Spain? Was that why he had gone to the scene of the crash? His hand touched the bruise on his forehead. The man he had fought with – the two men asking for him at the hotel in the mountains, and the gunman in his bedroom in Barcelona. They were the opposition, he thought, and they were after something. Something he was supposed to have got from the crash! Well, perhaps he had got something after all, he thought. Perhaps he had not. He didn't know whether he had or hadn't, and he wouldn't know until his memory came back to him. But the opposition didn't know that. They didn't know that he was suffering from amnesia. They thought he had something and was hiding from them. So he would just have to play them a waiting game until his memory came back to him, and keep out of their way.

An hour later, Stack was still in the café. He had gone over what ground he could recall. There were still many blanks, but he knew most of the score. He knew that the numbness inside of him was caused through a feeling of guilt and loneliness. Guilt at his part in the death of Emil Berak, and the loneliness caused by his job. He had become a pawn of British Intelligence, and he had become obsessed with his mission, even to the extent of losing Sue. And he was still involved. He was in Barcelona suffering from a partial loss of memory, and he knew that he was still involved. He also knew that he was on his own. When things had gone wrong in Berlin, Stack and his Control had separated. British Intelligence had to protect their organisation, and Stack's contacts had become suspect. But Stack had refused to lay off. Berak's contact in the East German Foreign Office had got on to something big. Something that would make up for all their setbacks. So Stack had been allowed to carry on alone. He had been left with an emergency link through British Military Intelligence in Berlin and a post box to his Control, but there was to be no physical contact with his Control. Stack had become a security risk.

Stack had gone it alone because he was made that way. He had to see it through to the end. He had fouled up his marriage. There had to be something worthwhile come out of it. So he had pushed Berak past the point of no return, and when Berak had wanted to escape there was no one Stack could turn to for help. Berak had got wind of an organisation that helped refugees escape to the West. Stack had made enquiries about it. He had gone looking for the organisation. Max Schafer had put him on to Hendrich Lieffer, the Berlin Director of the Ministry of Refugees. But Lieffer hadn't been able to help. No one had. Finally Berak had made his own contact with the organisation. He had prepared his own escape, and he had been shot, dead, in the attempt.

Stack was remembering fast, but not fast enough. He didn't remember what Gunter had passed to him from their contact, after he had taken over from Berak, or if they had arranged to meet in Barcelona, but he knew that there was an urgency, that something was imminent. He had to get his memory back, and he had to get to Berlin. But how, he wondered? How? He couldn't afford the time to tangle with the police, and he couldn't take on the opposition single-handed. He needed help to get out of Spain, but there was no one he could turn to without exposing himself to the dangers of the gunmen again. No one, he thought, except perhaps the man who had telephoned him – Doctor Lorenzo. He thought back to his telephone conversation with the doctor. The doctor's name, or voice, meant nothing to him. The man was a stranger, but his warning about the police had been timely enough, and the man had suggested that they could be of mutual assistance to each other. It could be a trap, he thought. The man could be working for the opposition, but on the other hand, the man might be on the level. He gave it plenty of thought. He couldn't think of an acceptable alternative suggestion, and he needed medical advice about his loss of memory. He finally decided to pay Lorenzo a visit, and find out just what the doctor had in mind by mutual assistance.

2

Stack found Doctor Lorenzo's surgery. It was in the heart of the dock area. He also found the doctor expecting him. As he stepped on to the last tread of the creaking staircase that discouraged malingerers from the doctor's surgery, a booming voice called out in English.

'You're late, Señor Stack, very late.'

Stack frowned. He didn't like being taken for granted. It annoyed him. He passed through an open glass-panelled door into a waiting-room that smelt of perspiring bodies. The walls were a dirty grey which hinted that once they had been white. The bench seats looked functional, but uncomfortable.

'Come in, Señor Stack,' the voice boomed again, from an inner room.

Stack passed through the waiting-room and stood at the entrance to the surgery. Sitting at a desk facing him was a large, fat figure with a perspiring face.

The face was round, heavy-jowled, beady-eyed and red. Perched on top of the head was a white, linen, trilby hat.

The two men eyed each other. Stack saw the soiled linen suit, but also the expensive silk shirt, the gold tie pin, gold cuff links and the gold watch.

'You're late,' the man boomed, 'and I do not normally remain in my surgery during the siesta period.'

Stack watched the doctor as he spoke. He sat, confidently overflowing from his chair, his eyes fixed on Stack, and his hand occasionally swishing a fly swat across his face.

'Doctor Lorenzo?' Stack asked.

'Yes,' Lorenzo replied. 'Disappointed?'

Stack shrugged and looked around the room. It was an improvement on the waiting-room. The furniture was respectable, the cabinets and fittings typical of a doctor's surgery. Only the floor was bare, like the waiting-room.

'Why do you ask?' Stack said calmly.

'You're frowning,' Lorenzo replied.

'I might have reasons,' Stack suggested.

'Not might,' Lorenzo said forcibly. 'Have.'

'You seem to know a lot,' Stack growled.

'Suppose you sit down,' Lorenzo said, and waved his arms impatiently. 'You make me feel uncomfortable, standing glowering at me.'

Stack sat down. Lorenzo opened a drawer, produced two glasses and a bottle of Cognac.

'French,' he boomed.

He poured out two drinks and gave one to Stack. He raised his glass and drank the cognac. Stack did the same.

'You understand that it is not for many men that I would remain in this stinking hole during siesta time,' Lorenzo said.

'You must want my help badly,' Stack said suspiciously.

'I do,' Lorenzo agreed, 'but I think you need my help just as badly.'

'Meaning?'

'The police,' Lorenzo said casually. 'They would like to question you.'

'Your spies have been busy.'

'Haven't they? But then, you were late arriving.'

'What are the police after?' Stack asked grimly.

Lorenzo shrugged. 'Some incident in the mountains,' he said.

'I don't know anything,' Stack replied.

'Don't remember anything, you mean,' Lorenzo suggested.

'You seem to be very well informed,' Stack said sourly.

'I try to be,' Lorenzo replied. 'What I don't know, I deduce.'

'Such as?'

'Your lost memory, for instance,' Lorenzo suggested.

Stack gave nothing away. If the doctor was only guessing, then Stack wasn't going to make him as wise as himself.

'My informants paid a call at the Hotel

San Miguel this morning,' Lorenzo added. 'We are not all simple peasants, Señor Stack. Nor was the young waiter.' He smiled patiently. 'The telephonist at the Hotel Excelsior is also one of my informers. Need I say more?'

Stack grunted noncommittally.

'Tell me about the police,' he said.

'In due time,' Lorenzo replied. 'Let us see if I can help you, professionally, first.'

'And then?'

'We talk business.'

The two men eyed each other. Stack wondered what Lorenzo was after. Whom he was working for. How far he could be trusted.

'Go and lie on the settee,' Lorenzo ordered. 'I will first examine you physically. Then we can talk about the mind.'

Stack hesitated.

'Come, Señor Stack,' Lorenzo boomed authoritatively. 'I am a doctor and you are suffering from a form of amnesia.'

Begrudgingly Stack took off his jacket and unbuttoned his shirt. Lorenzo lifted his bulk out of his chair and puffed his way across the room like a huge elephant. He sat on a ridiculous small stool next to Stack and poured his fleshy body over him. But his examination, although slow and ponderous, was also thorough. Finally, he puffed and grunted his way back to his desk and spread himself in, and over, his chair.

'Physically you are all right,' he said quietly. 'There are abrasions to your temple and the back of your skull. They will heal in due course.'

Stack dressed again and sat on the seat facing the doctor.

'You will be suffering from headaches,' Lorenzo added. 'They will pass shortly.'

'And the amnesia?' Stack asked. There was no point in trying to deny it, he thought. Lorenzo knew of his conversation with Max Schafer, and he had to know how bad his condition was.

Lorenzo put his podgy hands together.

'You received a blow to the head – when?'

Stack shrugged. 'Last night, probably.'

'Probably?' Lorenzo asked. 'Where?'

Stack shook his head.

'You can't remember, or you don't want to tell me?' Lorenzo asked.

'Can't remember,' Stack sighed. 'I awoke this morning in a strange bedroom with a loss of memory.'

'How much of a loss of memory?'

Stack looked thoughtful.

'I can remember things up to a couple of weeks, or so, ago. Little things are coming back. I can see faces and remember names, but there is a blank.'

'And after the incident that caused the injury to your head?'

'I must have acted rather vaguely. I made my way to a hotel. The waiter thinks I had too much to drink. I remember nothing until this morning.'

'And after this morning?'

'Everything's quite clear.'

'Even details?'

'Yes,' Stack frowned. 'It is only this blockage, of the past two weeks or so.'

'Does it coincide with any particular event that you know of?'

Stack didn't answer, and then looked away. 'Perhaps,' he said finally.

'Tell me about it.'

Stack shook his head. Lorenzo didn't try again.

'Okay,' Stack said. 'Let's have it, Doctor. You tell me – about amnesia.'

Lorenzo let his face rest on his chest for a short while, then he lifted it up and looked directly at Stack as if he were about to deliver a lecture.

'Amnesia can be caused by any condition which affects the consciousness,' he said. 'For instance, the use of drugs, or intoxication, can produce varying degrees of consciousness. Organic states such as epilepsy, or head injury, can also cause a disturbance. So can emotional stress and psychosis. In your case, you are suffering from both post traumatic amnesia and retrograde amnesia – loss of memory of events after, and before, the incident causing the disorder – caused quite simply by a blow, or a series of blows, to your head. Post traumatic amnesia is not uncommon. It is happening all the time. A person is knocked unconscious and during his period of recovery there may be this confusion, although the person may well act in what, to the onlooker, is normal behaviour. This, presumably, has happened to you. You acted and behaved in a normal manner, perhaps a little hazy, but you have done things over the past twelve hours or so which do not now register with you. You went to a hotel and remained overnight. That is your period of post traumatic amnesia. There has been a lot of evidence put forward to support the theory that the length of this type of amnesia is related to the extent of brain injury. If we accept that suggestion, and I am inclined so to do, we deduce that your head injuries are not of a serious nature.'

'That's some consolation,' Stack said seriously. 'That explains my loss of memory of events over the past few hours, but what about the other events?'

'Retrograde amnesia is often linked with post traumatic amnesia, but the period of retrograde amnesia is usually very short – a few seconds, minutes, perhaps hours. It is usually only with severe brain injury where retrograde amnesia may be of days, weeks or months.'

Stack shuffled about in his seat.

'That is not your condition,' Lorenzo added hastily.

'But I have a loss of memory of the events of the past few weeks,' Stack growled.

'I do not dispute that,' Lorenzo replied, 'so we must look for another cause.'

'Another cause?'

'Amnesia may also be psychogenic. In most cases where retrograde amnesia has exceeded the normal periods of time it has been regarded as largely psychogenic. A state of mind which causes a loss of memory. It can be brought on by great strain or stress, or a deep emotional state.'

'Such as a feeling of guilt?' Stack asked. He was thinking of Berak.

'It is possible,' Lorenzo agreed. 'A guilt complex can produce a form of self-punishment amnesia. The majority of loss of memory cases that come to the press are a result of some form of stress producing this psychogenic amnesia. It is a type of amnesia that often faces the courts of all countries. Many criminals plead this loss of memory.' He gave a faint smile. 'The subject offers itself to a deep study,' he added.

'So your diagnosis, Doctor,' Stack said thoughtfully, 'is that I am suffering from a form of amnesia caused by a blow to my head and an emotional stress.'

'The brain is a wondrous machine,' Lor-

41

enzo replied. 'It is something we do not fully comprehend. In my opinion it is not wise to generalise too much. We are all individuals with different brains, different minds, different emotions, and different strains. Your temporary loss of memory was caused by the blow to your head. It is most likely coupled with some strain which has found a means of expressing itself. There was a vacuum, it moved in, but the condition will pass.'

'When?' Stack asked anxiously. 'How long?'

'It could be minutes, hours, days,' Lorenzo replied. 'Treatment could accelerate the process. You could…'

'No, thanks,' Stack said firmly.

He couldn't allow himself to be subjected to any form of treatment that would make him confide his knowledge. He was working alone.

'In that case,' Lorenzo said, 'I suggest rest, no excitement. Return to your familiar surroundings. Your memory will come back. The brain mechanism which activates your memory has dried up for the want of a drop of oil. One day you will start providing some lubricant for it. You will get islands of memories. It will happen all the time. And who can tell? Some small happening – an object, action, or even a remark, might spark it all off. But there is still the emotional cause. That is something you want to try and be honest with yourself about.'

'So, it will come back,' Stack said quietly.

'It will come back,' Lorenzo agreed. 'It would be better if you talked about it. If you allow me to question you, we might make a bit of progress. We might even...'

'No!' Stack snapped. 'No.'

'I am a doctor.'

Stack was not impressed. He shook his head.

'No,' he said grimly. 'It will have to take its own course.'

'So be it,' the doctor replied.

The two men sat and looked at each other. The clicking fan at the window gave up its battle with the stale air and stopped, the motor finally beaten by the dust and dirt. The hot air seemed to weigh down on the two men. They sat in silence. The fan suddenly started again, the damaging particle of dust having been ground smaller. The stale, foul air moved again. The two men relaxed. Stack sat back, deflated. Lorenzo produced a packet of cigarellos from his inside pocket and silently offered one to Stack. Stack shook his head in refusal. He had lost his desire to smoke. Lorenzo lit his own cigarello and blew thick smoke into the room. It made the air fouler, but scented.

Neither man spoke for some time. Even when Lorenzo filled the two glasses and they drank the cognac, they still remained silent.

It was Stack who finally made the first move.

'Why do the police want me?' he asked quietly.

Lorenzo shrugged. 'There is a body of a man in the mountains,' he said, in an off-hand manner. 'A car ran off the road. You might not be involved, of course. It appears to have been an accident.'

Body! Car off the road! Stack felt his hand going to the back of his head and stopped himself.

'Was it near the scene of the air crash?' he asked.

'It was,' Lorenzo agreed.

Again Stack had to control himself from giving a visible sign of his concern.

'What if I give myself up?' he asked.

'Very noble.'

'And wise?'

Again Lorenzo shrugged. 'That depends upon how much you value your time,' he said. 'The police are unsympathetic, and their enquiries are slow. You would be required to remain in Barcelona for perhaps a few weeks.'

And he couldn't afford the delay, Stack thought. He knew that, but did the doctor also?

'So what do you suggest?' he asked.

'That is for you to decide,' Lorenzo replied, 'but certainly you will recover your memory quicker in Berlin than Barcelona. Your friends there will help you. You will find your islands of memories.'

'Why Berlin?' Stack asked suspiciously.

'That is where you have come from,' Lorenzo replied calmly.

Stack grunted. Lorenzo seemed to know a lot about him – a hell of a lot.

'And how do I do that?' Stack asked. 'The police will be watching the airport and border controls.'

Lorenzo gave a satisfied smile.

'I do not work in this hole without acquiring certain friends,' he said. 'There is a boat sailing tonight for Marseilles. Tomorrow night you could be there. From Marseilles you can fly to Berlin.'

'Very neat,' Stack replied, and thought that it was too neat.

'Yes,' Lorenzo agreed. 'It is.'

Stack breathed heavily.

'What's the catch?'

'The catch?' Lorenzo asked.

'We have never mentioned the price,' Stack said.

Lorenzo smiled.

'No,' he boomed.

'So?'

'So there is a price. I said I wanted to do business with you. Before your trouble I would have offered you money. Now I offer you your escape as well.'

'What do you want of me?' Stack asked suspiciously.

Lorenzo put his hands together as if in prayer.

'You know your way around Berlin?' he asked.

'Maybe,' Stack replied.

'I have a special friend who has need of a companion,' Lorenzo explained.

'Companion?'

'Someone who knows Berlin and who can act on my friend's behalf.'

'I have lost my memory, remember?' Stack growled. 'Perhaps I have forgotten Berlin also.'

'I don't think so,' Lorenzo said patiently.

Stack frowned. 'Let's have it,' he said. 'All of it.'

Lorenzo smiled. Stack didn't like the smile. It was one of satisfaction.

'I have naturally many contacts,' Lorenzo said, 'and interests.' He dropped his head on to his chest and looked at Stack with upturned eyes. 'And my special friend wants to get to Berlin to arrange for the escape of, shall we say, a Mister X from East Germany.'

'Escape! Who the hell do you think I am?'

'A man who knows his way around Berlin,' Lorenzo replied calmly, 'and who can speak fluent German.'

'Who told you that?'

'I made a few enquiries about you,' Lor-

46

enzo smiled, 'when I heard you had arrived at the Hotel Excelsior.'

'What the hell do you mean, a few enquiries?' Stack asked angrily.

'I have friends in many quarters,' Lorenzo said patiently, 'including the Press. One of them spoke very highly of you.'

'Who?' Stack asked.

'Señor Padreso,' Lorenzo replied calmly. 'You know him, of course.'

'I know him,' Stack agreed. Padreso was a respected member of the Spanish Press. He was a nomad of the Press circuit. His caravan appeared wherever there was international news. He was often in Berlin.

'You met him in Berlin on May 9th,' Lorenzo remarked, 'when the Federal German Chancellor entertained the Press. Agreed?'

Stack nodded his head in agreement.

'And he was entertained in your office by your editor in chief.'

'Okay,' Stack said. 'You have made your point. I know Padreso.' And he could check if Padreso had, in fact, given Lorenzo his name, he thought.

'He is a close friend,' Lorenzo explained, 'and he is also at this moment in Barcelona.' He heaved his heavy frame on to the desk and looked directly at Stack. 'I need someone who knows Berlin well. Someone who has perhaps access to both sides of the Wall. Someone who can be trusted. Señor

Padreso assures me that you are that person. That is all, Señor Stack. That is all. Don't read anything else into it.'

The two men looked hard at each other. Perhaps Lorenzo was telling the truth, Stack thought. Padreso was a man to be trusted. Maybe Lorenzo could also be trusted, and maybe he was just a good liar. Stack decided to keep an open mind.

Lorenzo sat back in his seat. 'My friend means a lot to me,' he said. 'She is from Israel.'

'She!'

'Yes – she.' Lorenzo put his fat, podgy hands together. 'I helped her mother many years ago. Now this young lady needs my help.'

'Well, you've picked the wrong boy,' Stack said. 'I have no contacts, or knowledge, of East Berlin, or East Germany.'

Lorenzo shuffled himself forward again and ferreted about with the papers on his desk. Finally he found what he wanted. It was an old issue of *Time* magazine. He flung it across the desk in front of Stack. Stack understood why. Inside was an article written by Stack referring to life in Berlin on both sides of the Wall. He had written it several months earlier on Max Schafer's urging.

'Okay,' Stack growled, 'but I still have no contacts with escape organisations.'

'It is of no consequence,' Lorenzo replied. 'We have the contacts. We know of such an organisation.'

Stack looked up sharply, his interest deeply aroused.

'You know of an organisation?' he asked. Berak had used such an organisation, he thought. Stack had even gone to Lieffer about it.

'Wherever there is a demand, and people are prepared to pay,' Lorenzo boomed, 'there will be a service provided.'

'Tell me about this organisation,' Stack asked.

Lorenzo smiled. 'Interested?' he asked.

'Perhaps,' Stack replied.

'I am going to be very honest with you, Señor Stack,' Lorenzo said. 'When our Civil War ended, I became part of an organisation that helped people get out of Spain.' He smiled patronisingly. 'I kept my contacts. For a long period of time I even helped refugees get to Palestine. I became part of a chain that started in Berlin. I have since turned my interests elsewhere, but I believe I can make contact with this organisation in Berlin, if it still exists, and I am told that it does.'

It certainly does, Stack thought. It certainly does.

'I take it you agree?' Lorenzo asked.

Agree! He had no alternative but to agree,

Stack thought. He had to get away from Barcelona and he had to get to Berlin. Lorenzo was offering him the opportunity to do both.

'Yes, I agree,' he replied grimly. The possibility of making contact with the organisation was a bonus attraction, he thought. Someone inside such an organisation had been responsible for Berak's murder. There wouldn't be two such organisations. It would be the same one. He was glad he had visited the doctor. Very glad.

'How do I contact them?' he asked.

'They will contact you.'

'Me!'

'Yes, you, my friend.'

Lorenzo had it all worked out, Stack thought.

'I am still a little curious as to why your friend hasn't got some of her own people to help her,' he remarked.

'She has in Berlin,' Lorenzo replied, 'but the man is elderly. Besides, she came to me for help, and I am a little old-fashioned. We Spanish are like that. I will feel happier if she has a chaperon, and after what Señor Padreso has told me about you...' He smiled and left the rest unsaid.

Stack grunted. It was a habit of his whenever he was confronted with some uncertainty.

'What about this?' he asked, touching the

bruise on his forehead. 'Doesn't that worry you?'

'No,' Lorenzo replied calmly. 'It does not.'

Again Stack grunted. He was beginning to think that Lorenzo had all the answers off a little bit too glib for his liking.

Lorenzo seemed to sense his agitation.

'I know just enough about you, Señor Stack,' he boomed, 'to know that our business arrangement can succeed. I don't wish to know more. After you leave Barcelona, you never existed. You understand?'

'I understand,' Stack replied. There was to be no scratching beneath the surface, he thought. No questions. It was a one off, business deal.

'And when do I meet your friend?' he asked.

'Tonight. Be in this room at ten p.m. You will sail on the *Fleur de Lyon* which leaves for Marseilles at midnight.'

'And what am I supposed to do until tonight?' Stack asked. 'Or have you got that planned as well?'

'Do what you will,' Lorenzo replied. 'There is a bar and a café next door. You will be safe there, and you will find several girls prepared to help you spend your time, but if you take my advice, you will leave them alone.' He stood up and shuffled to the door, and held it ajar for Stack. Their meeting was over. 'There is also my waiting-room at your

51

disposal,' Lorenzo added. 'I prefer to keep my surgery locked.'

'I think the cheapest of the brothels would be preferable to your waiting-room,' Stack remarked dryly.

Lorenzo's face gave the faintest flicker of a smile.

'Then you haven't been in the very cheapest,' he replied. His face became serious again. 'But as you wish,' he said.

Stack left the surgery and slowly descended the creaking staircase. It had been an interesting visit, he thought, very interesting. Life had suddenly taken on another dimension.

It was bright, hot and noisy in the area surrounding Lorenzo's surgery. Stack knew that he had to keep himself hidden until darkness came. The opposition and the police could both be looking for him. He found a small, private boarding house which was marginally preferable to Lorenzo's waiting-room. It offered a room with a bed, and an opportunity to get some privacy and rest. He took the room and got the rest. When he later made his way back to the doctor's surgery, he felt better equipped to handle anything that came his way. He also felt suspicious and curious about Lorenzo's motives. The doctor had put up a very plausible case for soliciting Stack's help. He was also providing Stack with the two very things that Stack wanted most – a quick, secret exit from Barcelona, and an introduction to the organisation in Berlin that helped refugees to escape from East Germany. Lorenzo had suddenly come into Stack's life like a fairy godmother – but Stack didn't believe in fairies!

The staircase leading to the surgery was in darkness when Stack entered the building, and there was no light shining from the surgery door, but as Stack opened the waiting-room door, he smelled the fragrance of the doctor's cigarellos and knew that the doctor was in his room. Stack opened the surgery door, and in the moonlight saw the doctor sitting, smoking, at his desk.

'You are prompt,' Lorenzo said. 'I like that.'

Stack closed the door behind him. There was a slim, dark-clothed figure sitting on a chair alongside the door. It was a girl. She sat, stiff backed, in a timid, anxious pose. Two huge, white eyes looked at Stack from beneath a dark beret. Stack turned to Lorenzo.

'Your friend?' he asked.

'She is the person you are going to look after,' Lorenzo agreed, emphasising the words as if Stack had made some grammatical error.

'What have you told her about me?' Stack asked.

'Sufficient,' Lorenzo replied. 'She knows

about your partial loss of memory.'

'But she still goes?' Stack asked.

'It is of no concern to her,' Lorenzo replied.

'I still go, Mr Stack,' the girl said quietly, in English.

Stack swung around to see her standing up. She came up to his shoulder. He saw her two dark eyes looking at him.

'What is your name?' he asked.'

'Lehna Rosier,' she said.

'And why do you want help in Berlin?'

'My fiancé is in hiding in East Berlin. I want to arrange for his escape, so that we can return together to Israel.'

'So you came to Barcelona?' Stack asked suspiciously.

'She came to see me,' Lorenzo boomed.

Stack turned to face him.

'She came to see me,' Lorenzo said again, 'because I helped her mother to escape from Germany, and I brought Lehna into the world, twenty-three years ago.'

'Then why didn't you advise her to remain in Israel and marry someone else?' Stack asked.

'That is not the way of my family,' Lehna said. She turned to the doctor and spoke to him in Spanish. She spoke very fast, but Stack got the gist of the conversation. She was asking Lorenzo if there was no one else who could help her. When she had finished,

54

Lorenzo turned to Stack.

'You understood what she was saying?' he asked.

'Some,' Stack replied.

'I am sorry I spoke in Spanish,' the girl said to Stack. 'I did not wish to offend you. I have the feeling that you do not wish to help me.'

'It might prove dangerous for your friend,' Stack growled.

Lorenzo snorted impatiently.

'Enough of this talk,' he growled. 'You will have to leave for the ship. The second mate will take care of you.'

'As easy as that,' Stack said irritably.

'As easy as that,' Lorenzo agreed impatiently. 'Come, Señor Stack, we are men of the world. It happens all the time. Besides, you have a passport. With you there is no problem.' He opened a drawer and threw some French money on to the table. 'This will get you from Marseilles to Berlin,' he said.

Stack picked up the money.

'You meet Lehna in Marseilles,' Lorenzo explained. 'At the Hotel de France, Rue de Rouen. It is close to the docks.'

'How is she getting there?' Stack asked.

'By rail.'

'And how long do I wait?'

'You won't have to,' the girl snapped. 'I will be waiting for you.'

'You must go now,' Lorenzo boomed. 'Good night, Señor Stack.'

Stack looked at the huge frame of the doctor and the slim figure of the girl. He felt that he was being propelled into a situation that had been carefully planned for him. But he also felt that he wanted to go through with it. And the attraction was the organisation in Berlin. The organisation that had sent Berak to his death.

3

The *Fleur de Lyon* was a cargo ship which had seen a lot of service. The quarters that Stack was given had also seen a lot of passengers, and from the markings on the bulkhead, it appeared that the ship was doing a steady trade in bringing coloured immigrants into Europe. Stack's quarters were filthy, stinking, and only just bearable, but the enforced detention helped to restore some of his injuries. He slept soundly and long. When he awoke, he felt more capable of sorting out what fitted and what was missing. He knew a little more about himself and his double role, but there was still the impasse after Berak had been killed. Berak, Gunter, and Stack. That had been the triangle in Berlin. Berak, the link with the contacts in the Communist hierarchy, and Gunter the reserve. Stack and Berak had met whenever there was a gathering of Press correspondents, or whenever Berak had some information to give him. Stack would then pass it on to Control, but after the arrests and failures Stack's link with Control had been severed. They still watched over him like an invisible, mothering hen, but they remained hidden in the shadows. Stack was on his own, with only a post box, and an emergency link through a Major Roberts of Military Intelligence – a man known to the K.G.B. and Western Intelligence agencies alike. Stack's post box, and codes, were simple, but effective, using the underworld of Berlin that feeds on the spy network like the drones of a beehive. They had their short-term uses, but their long-term allegiances were suspect. Like Stack, they were expendable.

Stack also thought about Doctor Lorenzo and Lehna Rosier. They had suddenly become part of his life. They had got him out of Spain and they were using him in Berlin. He was by nature suspicious of everything, and Lorenzo remained high up on his priority list.

It was after midnight when Stack left the ship in Marseilles. In the darkness, the dockside buildings, streets and cafés looked similar to those in Barcelona. Only the signs and names were different.

As he left the immediate area of the docks, he felt that he was being followed. Several times he hid in the shadows of the buildings, but the figures that passed by meant nothing to him.

He found the Hotel de France in a narrow side street of tall buildings, where the balconies almost touched those opposite. The dimly lit entrance hallway didn't offer much encouragement for the standard of the hotel. The carpet was threadbare, and the reception counter was a piece of unfinished joinery of another generation.

Stack knocked on the counter, and the *patronne* came through a narrow doorway from a back room. She was elderly and robust, to the extent that she had to manoeuvre herself, gingerly, through the narrow door opening.

She looked at Stack from head to feet.

'We have no rooms,' she growled in French, shaking her head.

'I am already booked in,' Stack replied, in poor French. 'Mademoiselle Rosier.'

The proprietress looked at him sullenly. 'Number 36,' she said.

Stack climbed the narrow, winding staircase, with the eyes of the woman following him. As he went from floor to floor, voices penetrated the thin, wooden doors of the bedrooms.

Lehna's room on the very top floor of the building.

Stack knocked, quietly, on the door.

'Who is it?' Lehna called out in French.

'Stack.'

'Come in.'

Stack opened the door and entered the room. It was lit by a single electric light bulb that gave a dull, yellow glow.

59

Lehna was sitting on an iron-framed bed, fully clothed, a book and her handbag by her side. She gave a faint smile of welcome.

Stack closed the door behind him and looked around the room. It was an improvement on his previous quarters. There was the iron-posted bed, a divan, a cupboard, and a worn carpet on the floor.

'How was the journey?' Lehna asked.

'Stinking,' Stack replied.

'This is not much better,' she said apologetically.

'It is better, though,' he said, and came into the centre of the room where he could see her more clearly. She was wearing a simple, navy blue dress which made her appear very slim. Her bare arms and legs were deeply tanned. So was her face.

She smiled, showing white, even teeth. She looked so young, he thought, almost childlike. Her eyes were deep brown, surrounded by white. They were soft eyes, so was her mouth, and her hair was dark brown, short and neat. She had a gentle face, but Stack had known other women who had soft, gentle looks, but who had also been as hard as iron. There was no reason to think that this one would be any different, he thought. He weighed up the rest of what he saw. The full bosom, the shapely, youthful body. Now that did appeal to him, he thought. With that there would be no mistrust.

'Do you always have to mentally strip your women?' she snapped.

'Only if they appeal,' Stack replied, and looked away.

'You look tired and hungry,' she said, with less irritation.

'I am tired,' he agreed, and caught sight of himself in the mirror. His face was black with his beard; his eyes red rimmed.

'And hungry?' she asked. 'I have some rolls and cheese.'

'That would be fine.'

She produced the food from a bag and gave it to him.

'How do you feel?' she asked hesitantly. 'Do you...'

'My memory?' he asked.

'Yes.'

'I have remembered some,' he replied.

'That is good.'

He looked up at her.

'Why should it concern you?' he asked.

'It doesn't,' she retorted. 'I was being sociable.'

Stack grunted. 'What makes you so sure that I can help you?' he asked. 'The doctor?'

She dropped her eyes.

'Yes,' she said.

'He referred to an organisation,' Stack said, eating the food. 'Tell me all you know about it.'

'I don't know very much,' she said. 'All I

know is from my friends, and what my mother told me about it. It helped Jewish refugees from the displaced camps to get to Palestine.'

'Go on.'

'There isn't much else. The organisation originated in Berlin, but it has spread far afield.'

'For free?'

She shook her head.

'No,' she said sadly. 'They charged a lot of money. Some families could not afford to pay for all of the family to go to Israel, so they split up, hoping to pay for their remaining relatives when they got work in Israel.'

'And you?'

'There was only my mother. My father died before I was born, from the effects of his imprisonment.'

'And your mother is in Israel?'

'No. She died two years ago.'

Again Stack grunted.

Lehna got off the bed and went over to the dormer window. She wrapped her arms around herself as if she was cold.

'We lived in a Kibbutz with other people,' she said, her back to Stack, 'but it was still lonely. When Paul wrote to say that he was going to East Berlin to try and arrange to get to Israel, I immediately thought of Doctor Lorenzo. My mother had told me about Doctor Lorenzo. I wrote to Paul and told him that I would help him.'

'Did you also write to the doctor?'

'Yes. He told me to come to Barcelona.'

She turned to face him.

'So I arrived, two days ago, and you arrived yesterday. It was very fortunate for me.'

'Perhaps,' Stack muttered. Her story was simple and touching. He was suitably moved, but still sceptical enough to wonder if that had been the object of the exercise.

'Tell me about your fiancé,' he said. 'What's he like? What's his background?'

'His name is Paul Criller,' she replied, without hesitation. 'He is twenty-six years of age. He is a little smaller than you in height and wears spectacles. He is short-sighted. Oh, he is dark, good looking, with jet black hair. He lived in Leipzig with his mother. He is an engineer.'

'Was the marriage arranged?'

'Yes,' she said, without any sign of regret. 'It is the way of my people. Our parents were friends. They were together in a concentration camp.'

'And Criller is now in East Berlin?'

'Yes. We have an emissary in West Berlin. His name is Franz Hessler. He has been in contact with Paul.'

'Good,' Stack said. 'That should help.'

She smiled at him.

'You know all about me now,' she said. 'Is

there anything I should know about you? Are you married, for instance?'

Stack frowned and looked away.

'I was until nine months ago,' he growled. 'My wife and I parted company.'

'Oh!' she said. 'I'm sorry.'

Stack didn't want to talk about it. He looked at his watch as an excuse.

'It is late,' he said. 'We have talked enough for tonight.'

He stood up, and looked at the bed and the divan in the alcove.

'This was the only room available,' she said apologetically.

'The divan will do me fine,' he said.

She handed him a pillow and one of the blankets. He didn't bother to wash. He felt that to have done so would have disturbed the whole of the plumbing system in the building. He took off his blue jacket and made himself comfortable.

Presently the light went out.

'Good night,' Lehna said quietly.

'Good night,' Stack replied.

He lay facing the wall, his brain trying to lift the veil. He felt it was very close, almost within his grasp, but he drifted into the realms of sleep without becoming any closer.

Suddenly he was awake, his pulse racing. There was danger! He felt it. Something had disturbed him. He lay quite still and heard a faint grating noise. Instantly he became

64

alert. He heard the noise again. It was the lock on their bedroom door being turned! He got out of bed. He was in a recess behind the door. He brought himself, quietly, to his full height and flattened himself on the side wall behind the door. The door very slowly opened, and with it came the sickly fragrance of strong, scented perfume.

A faint light fell into the room from a window on the landing, silhouetting the iron-framed bed and the still figure of Lehna.

Stack held his breath and edged himself along the face of the opened door. He saw a man's figure moving towards the bed. Stack moved slowly forward. The intruder flashed a torchlight on the figure in the bed. Stack stepped back. The beam came to rest on Lehna's face, where it remained, momentarily, and was then extinguished. The man edge himself away from the bed, back to the open doorway.

Stack took a deep breath. When the man was in the doorway, Stack made his move. With all the force he could muster, he slammed the door into the man's back. There was an anguished groan as the door collided with its object and forced the man against the door jamb. Stack pulled the door open, saw the bent figure of the man, and lunged on top of him. Together, they collapsed on to the unpolished landing. There was an instant cry of an excited voice and the landing lights came on.

Stack picked himself up and grabbed the man by the lapels of his jacket. He swung him around and crashed him into the bedroom wall. He felt a rain of blows on his back and heard a woman's voice. In front of him he saw a frightened face and two eyes staring at him. He brought his arm back to lash at the face in front of him. Somebody held his arm back.

'No!'

It was the proprietress. Stack pulled his arm free.

'No!' the proprietress cried again.

Stack saw Lehna in the doorway. There was a worried look on her face. He let his arm go limp. There was an excited gabble of abuse from the proprietress. Stack turned and saw her gesticulating, angrily, at him. He turned his attention back to the figure he still held pinned against the wall. It was a dark-faced, wide-eyed man. His face was bleeding and he smelled of perfume. The perfume of pimps. Stack looked at the man's fancy clothes. The man was a pimp, he thought, or some other guttersnipe of the back streets.

He let go of the man's jacket and the man sank slowly to the floor. Again there came a rain of abuse from the proprietress, who only interrupted her flow of local adjectives to reply to some irate guests from the floor below.

'Is he all right?' Lehna asked anxiously. Stack looked at her. She was standing with a gown wrapped around her.

'Yes. He will be all right,' he said.

He picked the man up.

'Mercy,' the man cried in English.

'I'm not going to touch you,' Stack replied. He carried the man into the bedroom. The proprietress followed them. Stack looked at her. She returned the look defiantly, daring him to ask her to leave. Stack closed the door. Lehna went and sat on the bed and watched. Stack picked up the water basin, filled it from the pitcher, and threw the towel to the proprietress.

'Here,' he said. 'Help your friend. I want some answers before he leaves.'

The proprietress scowled openly as she accepted the towel. She wet it and wiped the man's face. Presently the man was able to do it himself. He doused himself and fastened his tie. He brought out a comb and straightened his sleek black hair. When he was satisfied with his appearance, he turned to Stack and said in English, 'A little too rough, I think.'

'I don't like intruders in the night,' Stack replied.

'I didn't intend to disturb you,' the man said apologetically. He had an effeminate voice, and his eyes blinked incessantly. Stack was relieved when the man collected a pair of sunglasses, and his trilby hat, from the proprietress, and put them both on.

'Why did you come?' Stack asked.

The man shrugged. 'It was a possibility,' he said.

'What was?'

'That the girl was someone I was looking for.'

'And is she?'

The man opened his hands, shrugged his shoulders regretfully, and sighed, 'I regret to say, no.'

'Perhaps, if you tell us who you are looking for, we might be able to help you,' Stack said.

The man gave a resigned gesture.

'That is not possible, Monsieur,' he said.

Stack moved pointedly towards him. The proprietress, and Lehna, gave an anxious start.

'Even if you attack me again, Monsieur,' the man said hurriedly, 'I would still not tell you. Even I have my honour.'

'Honour?' Stack asked.

'Does that surprise you, Monsieur?'

'What are you?' Stack asked. 'A thief? Crook? Smuggler? Procurer?'

'No, Monsieur,' the man replied, without offence. 'I am a private investigator. In America they call us private eyes. In your country, a private detective.'

'Private detective!' Stack exclaimed incredulously.

The proprietress and the man exchanged a quick burst of conversation.

'She wants to know if you are on the run,' the man said. He looked apologetic. 'She reads so many books,' he added. 'You understand?'

'No, I am not on the run,' Stack said forcibly, 'but tell her that she shouldn't allow you to have free access to her rooms.'

The man smiled and winced.

'Oh, she's not alone,' he said. 'It is my profession. She would have received a percentage of my reward if your friend had been the person I was looking for.'

Stack grunted.

'Well, she isn't,' he growled, 'and you can both clear out.'

'*Merci*, Monsieur,' the man smiled. 'Let me give you my card, just in case I can ever be of assistance to you.'

He withdrew a card from his inside pocket and politely handed it to Stack.

'One must always look for business,' he added, and turned to Lehna. 'I am indeed sorry you are not the person I am looking for,' he sighed. 'It would have saved so much time – and money.'

He moved to the door. Stack studied the card. M. Henri Gallon, he read, Private Investigator, 112 Rue de Sorbon, Marseilles.

'One moment,' he called out.

'Yes, Monsieur?'

The man hesitated in the doorway.

'How far do your connections stretch?' Stack asked.

'That depends on how much is being paid,' the man replied hurriedly.

'Let's say as far as Barcelona,' Stack suggested.

The man shrugged. 'Telephone calls can mount up, but I have an arrangement with a friend in Barcelona.'

'How long would it take you to find out something about a man who left Barcelona yesterday and arrived in Marseilles this evening?' Stack asked.

'If the man should have arrived on the *Fleur de Lyon*,' Gallon said airily, 'it would make it a simple matter.'

Stack grunted.

'You're on, Henri, old boy,' he said brightly. 'Have you got another card?'

The Frenchman produced another card.

Again the proprietress gesticulated with him.

'She says that you will not pay me,' the man said sadly.

Stack looked pointedly at the woman, who dropped her eyes. He went to his jacket and opened his wallet.

'Here are three hundred francs as initial expenses,' he said. He handed the money over to Gallon. 'There is more if you can get me the facts about these people.'

He gave Gallon back his card. On the reverse side he had written three names.

The Frenchman looked at the names and the instructions.

'Come to my office, at, say, ten tomorrow evening,' he said confidently. 'I will have something for you.'

'Your office?'

'It is on the card. It is above the Café Beyeux.'

'I'll be there,' Stack said.

The Frenchman smiled.

'*Au revoir*, Monsieur,' he said, and turned to Lehna. '*Au revoir*, Mademoiselle. It is such a pity you were not the person I was looking for.' He held his trilby above his head, and left the room followed by the proprietress.

'He is lucky to be alive,' Lehna said coldly when they were alone, 'after the way you attacked him.'

Stack frowned. He had let loose on the Frenchman because the man had come uninvited into their bedroom. No one did that to Stack and got away with it.

'He came into our room uninvited,' he snapped.

'Yes. He was in the wrong, but there was no need to treat him like that.'

Stack growled his disgust, put out the light, and returned to his divan.

'Whose names did you give him?' Lehna

asked in the darkness.

'Mine,' Stack replied, 'and Doctor Lorenzo's.'

'And mine?'

'Would it bother you?'

'Yes, it would,' Lehna snapped. 'I am in a hurry to get to Berlin, and I know all about myself and Doctor Lorenzo.'

'But I don't know all about myself,' Stack replied evenly, 'and we can still get to Berlin tomorrow night.'

Lehna muttered her disapproval.

Stack made himself comfortable. He had lashed out at the man in his hotel room in Barcelona as well as the Frenchman, he thought. Was he aggressive by nature, he wondered? Or was it frustration that was causing it? He shuffled about in his bed and forgot about it. Instead he thought about the Frenchman. If his contacts were as good as he boasted, then Stack might just find something out about himself – and about Lorenzo and the girl.

Stack slept fitfully. His mind kept reminding him of the need to find out why Gunter had been on the plane that had crashed. He awoke to see the sun streaming through the window and Lehna missing. He got out of bed and felt drowsy, his head thick and heavy. But he knew where he was and what had taken place. His mind quickly explored the past and stopped at the same impasse –

the blank weeks after Gunter had taken over. He wondered where Lehna had gone and how long she had been away. He also wondered why Lorenzo had been so enthusiastic for her to accompany him. Why they hadn't joined each other in Berlin.

He washed and shaved, and was packing his bag when Lehna returned.

'Just been exploring,' she explained cheerfully. She had changed into a colourful dress that made her look even more youthful than before. 'There is a café close by,' she said eagerly, 'where we can have breakfast.'

'Go and pay the bill,' Stack ordered. 'Then we will get away from here.'

'Away? Why?'

Stack stopped packing his bag.

'Look,' he said sternly. 'Dear Henri, last night, just happened to know which ship I had come from. It might just be the case that others will also know.'

'Others?' Lehna asked, frowning. 'Why should there be others?'

Because a gunman came into my hotel bedroom in Barcelona, Stack thought, and two men were looking for him in the mountains, but he didn't say that. Instead he asked, 'Did Lorenzo tell you that the Spanish police are looking for me?'

'Yes,' she replied.

'Well, we are still close enough to the Spanish border for me to be concerned. I have no love for the Spanish police, or their jails.'

Lehna shrugged. She didn't agree with him and it showed, but she went and paid the bill.

They left the hotel and Stack hurried her through the back streets into the adjoining district. When he was satisfied that they were not being followed, he took her to a small hotel that he had used before. It was on a busy thoroughfare close to the docks, but it was an improvement on their previous hotel. They took a room on the third floor with a view of the waterfront.

'And what do we do here?' Lehna asked irritably, when they were alone in the room.

'I am going to sit and enjoy the view,' Stack replied calmly, 'until it is time to visit dear old Henri. As for you...' He shook his head sadly, with mock concern. 'Now let me see. There is a sun terrace on the roof,' he said thoughtfully, 'and a restaurant on the ground floor. Which do you prefer?'

She snorted her dislike of the situation and left the room. Stack wasn't perturbed. He was more concerned about getting out of Marseilles in one piece than Lehna's tantrums. He ordered some breakfast, and made himself comfortable where he could watch what was happening in the street below. If he was going to have any unwelcome visitors, he would be ready to receive them.

But Stack was not disturbed. The day

passed without incident. It would also have passed slowly for him, if it hadn't been for Lehna. She soon lost her annoyance at being delayed, and provided him with some welcome relief from his vigil. She talked long and earnestly about her life as a teacher in the Kibbutz, and of her plans for the future. He enjoyed her company and was again impressed by her sincerity.

Shortly before ten p.m., they left the hotel and went in search of Henri Gallon. They picked up a taxi outside the hotel, and Stack told the driver to drive slowly past the Café Beyeux in the Rue de Sorbon.

There was a lot of traffic about; the cafés and bars were busy, the pavement tables occupied. The Rue de Sorbon also had its shops, bars and colourful neon signs. They approached the Café Beyeux. Stack saw the café front and the busy tables on the pavement. He looked for Gallon's office. Gallon had said it was above the café. There was no light shining from the windows, only the red neon sign on the wall above the café. Puzzled, Stack told the driver to stop at the far end of the street. They drove past the café. Stack looked up at the darkened windows and became suspicious. Gallon had said ten p.m. and it was then a minute after.

The taxi driver stopped the car.

'What are you going to do?' Lehna asked.

'I have an appointment with our friend,

Henri,' Stack replied. 'I'm going to keep it.'

'I'll come with you,' Lehna said.

'No,' Stack replied firmly. 'I'm going in the back way. You remain with the taxi.' He glanced at his watch. 'Give me exactly fifteen minutes, then drive up to the café and wait. I will either signal you from the office window to join me, or I will join you.'

He got out of the taxi before she had time to argue and walked quickly along the narrow lane that ran behind the Rue de Sorbon. It was dark, but he found the rear entrance of the café by stumbling into a number of foul-smelling dustbins. He entered a small yard and saw the brightly lit kitchen. Without hesitation, he entered the building and smiled politely at a woman who looked up at him questioningly. He picked his way through the kitchen tables, and felt the surprised eyes of the woman following him. Ahead of him were two doors. One opened and a waiter came through, shouting an order to the cook. He looked at Stack. Stack side-stepped him and took the other door. It brought him into a darkened passageway. He saw a staircase and the café tables on the pavement. He climbed the staircase. Gallon's office was on the first-floor landing. In the red glow from the neon sign, Stack read Gallon's name on the glass-panelled door. He turned the door handle – it responded. The door opened and Stack saw Gallon sitting at his desk. But it was a still, rigid Gallon. His eyes were wide open, his head hung to one side. He was dead! There was a neat hole in the middle of his temple where a bullet had killed him!

Stack's inside turned over and froze. Grimly he stood rooted to the spot, staring at the slim, still figure in the fancy suit. Gallon looked like a painted dummy; a puppet that had been propped into a chair. Stack stopped himself from lashing out at the furniture. Henri Gallon was dead because he had mistakenly come into Stack's bedroom looking for a missing girl. Gallon was dead because of Stack. Because Stack had asked him to seek out some information about Stack's movements. Stack was again to blame!

For several seconds Stack stood cursing himself and everyone. It was like a picture from hell. The red glow from the neon sign illuminating the room; the furniture and papers lying scattered on the floor, and Gallon's wide eyes staring – just staring.

Stack went over to the desk. It had been stripped bare. The drawers were empty and so were Gallon's pockets. Somebody had gone to a lot of bother to make sure that Stack didn't get to know anything. He heard a car drive up and stop outside the café. He went to the window and saw that it was the taxi. He also saw the figures sitting at the tables on the pavement, and wondered if Gallon's murderer was amongst them. He turned away and hurried out of the room and down the stairs.

As he picked his way through the tables to the taxi, Lehna opened the car door for him.

'Airport!' Stack shouted loudly, and got into the taxi.

The driver quickly pulled away. Stack sank into the seat. Lehna looked at him questioningly.

'Well?' she asked.

'Gallon was there all right,' Stack whispered, 'but someone got to him first.'

'No!' Lehna gasped hoarsely.

'He is dead,' Stack explained quietly. 'Shot in the head.'

'Oh! My God!' Lehna exclaimed.

Stack gripped her hand. She was shaking.

'I'm going to tell the driver to take us to the railway station,' he said.

'The railway station? But I thought we were gong to the airport.'

'So does everyone else,' Stack growled. 'Just in case, I think we will take the sleeper to Paris.'

He spoke to the driver, who shrugged his confusion and muttered under his breath. Lehna turned to Stack and looked at him appealingly.

'It must have been in connection with his other business,' Stack said encouragingly.

'Do you think so?' Lehna asked hesitantly. 'Honestly?'

'Sure,' Stack lied. 'There can be no other reason. Don't you worry yourself. We will soon be in Berlin and everything will work out okay.'

He squeezed her hand affectionately. The sooner they got to Berlin the better, he thought. In Berlin, he existed. He had status there that helped to protect him. He wasn't the nobody that he was in Marseilles. He also had his Control. If they knew of his dilemma they would give him a cover. He had to get a message to them through Roberts.

4

Stack and Lehna arrived at Tempelhof Airport, Berlin, in the afternoon following their night trip to Paris. Their journey from Marseilles had been tedious and uneventful, but nevertheless, Stack knew that the situation hadn't changed. The dangers were the same, only the ground and spectators were now going to be more to his liking. In Berlin, Stack felt the odds were not so heavily loaded against him.

When the passengers disembarked from the aircraft, Stack and Lehna parted company, to make their way independently to a hotel in Charlottenburg where Stack was known. Stack had put this suggestion to Lehna on the grounds that he wanted to be free to be approached by any of Lorenzo's contacts without her becoming involved. Fortunately, she had agreed without argument. His real reason for wanting to be on his own was to try and divorce Lehna from his own involvement, because of the danger of spill-off. For the same reason, he had decided against using his apartment in Kurfiersten Strasse, despite the advantages of being in familiar surroundings.

The airport terminal building was busy and noisy. Stack passed through the Customs and controls without hindrance. He lost Lehna amongst the sea of faces, and picked up a taxi in the ranks outside the terminal entrance. But he didn't make for the hotel; he headed into the heart of the city. In Paris he had sent a brief, coded message to Roberts of Military Intelligence, asking for protection. He wanted to establish this tenuous link with his Control. He also wanted to find out if the opposition were also keeping close to him.

As the taxi glided past the familiar landmarks of modern buildings glistening in the afternoon sun, Stack felt himself becoming more alive and confident, but his mind still held back the spring to release his memory bank. There was still a blank. He left the taxi at Kurfürstendamm, at the corner of Uhlandstrasse. It was Sunday afternoon. The traffic was not so busy as midweek and neither were the pavement cafés. He purchased a newspaper and sat at a table in a café that he used regularly. He ordered a coffee and turned his attention to his newspaper. The leading articles mainly dealt with the forthcoming visit of the Yugoslav President and the German Chancellor's attempt to build bridges between the East and West. He frowned as he read the reports. They were familiar to him, yet distant, as if they were just out of his grasp. It was something he knew about, but had forgotten the details.

He finished his coffee and set out to flush any tails. He paid the waiter and walked away from the café. From a shop window, he caught the reflection of the pedestrians behind him. Their faces registered. He increased his pace and became one of the masses. It didn't take him long to pick out his man. A short walk and trip on the Underground had flushed him. He was of medium height, slim, wearing a light-coloured suit. Not a man who stood out in a crowd, unless you took precautions. Stack continued with his antics, the man hung on and established himself as a cover. Stack looked for number two. He didn't find one. That meant the opposition were either out-smarting him, or hadn't joined the game yet. At five p.m. he gave up the first round and went to his hotel. Lehna was in her room waiting for him. She looked tense and on edge.

'I was worried,' she explained. 'You have been so long.'

Perhaps they were on to Lehna, he thought, and were by-passing him.

'What do we do?' Lehna asked anxiously.

'Wait until we are contacted,' Stack replied. 'It shouldn't be too long if Lorenzo has done his part. Why don't you go and see your friend, Franz Hessler? Find out what contact has been made with Criller.'

He wanted to be free that evening to see Max. He didn't want Lehna around, and he wanted to give the organisation an opportunity to make contact.

'Where shall we meet?' Lehna asked.

'In the cocktail bar,' Stack replied. 'Let's say about ten. We can dine then. That should give you plenty of time to get to Hessler's apartment and back.'

She smiled at him faintly.

'I never did say I was sorry,' she said apologetically.

'About what?'

'About doubting you in Marseilles,' she replied, and looked at him with her large eyes.

'That was because of Gallon's other business,' Stack said firmly.

'I hope so,' she sighed.

'Come on, we'll go and have a drink.'

They went to the lounge. Stack's cover was already there. Stack wondered how concerned Control were becoming. Whether they knew about his trouble. He ordered two drinks.

They sat and talked. Lehna became more at ease and more determined to do something constructive that would help. Stack assured her that visiting Hessler was important, and that they had to know how Criller could be contacted. He got her a taxi and she went on her visit. He felt that she was safe enough on her own. She was only the carrier, just as Lorenzo was the post box. If the organisation didn't want to help, they would just remain out of sight. It was Stack who interested someone – Henri Gallon had proved that.

He returned to the hotel and set about locating Max Schafer. He telephoned the office. It was staffed all week-end, but Schafer wasn't there. He tried some of the bars that Schafer used and found him at one of them. He left word that he was on his way and took a taxi. So did his cover. The man was beginning to irritate him because he wasn't using any finesse with his job. The opposition would pick him out a mile away.

Schafer was standing at the bar counter, a glass in his hand and a cigar in his mouth, when Stack arrived. Schafer always stood at the bar counter when he was drinking, Stack thought, and he always had a cigar in his mouth. He was a small, squat man, with a face that looked as if it had been lived with. It was weather-beaten, scraggy and expressive. A description which fitted Maximillian Schafer himself. Schafer was an American, of German descent, and his language and personality were a combination of the two worlds. He was a bachelor, steeped in journalism from the days of the Spanish Civil War, when he had first descended on Europe as a young, enthusiastic, photographic correspondent for a New York newspaper. He had never returned to the States. He had spent the war in Europe and afterwards moved into Berlin. He was a colourful character, both in his dress and in his personality – a character Stack liked. He was a professional at his job with a nose for news, and connections with roots stretching into every nook and corner of Europe. The two men were close, but their friendship was all on the front. They worked together, but lived separate lives, which gave Stack the freedom he required.

'Hell, it's good to see you, John,' Schafer said, shaking Stack's hand warmly. 'You had me worried on the telephone. When did you get back?'

'Today,' Stack replied. 'I've been on to the office.'

Schafer handed Stack a drink. 'Carlos has taken over in Barcelona,' he said. 'How do you feel?'

'Physically okay,' Stack said, 'but there is a bit of a blank.'

'Blank?'

'A couple of weeks or so missing. They'll come back.'

'Have you seen a doctor?'

'Saw one in Barcelona. You might know him. A man called Lorenzo.'

'Lorenzo?' Schafer asked, and repeated

the name thoughtfully. 'Lorenzo. Can't say I do,' he said.

Stack was surprised. He put Lorenzo in the same set of international eccentrics that Schafer belonged to.

'He's a bit of a character,' Stack said.

'What did he say?'

Stack took a drink. 'Nothing to worry about. The fog will clear in time. Something might start the wheels going again.'

'What caused it, John?'

'A blow to the head,' Stack replied. 'I must have tripped over something. Can't remember anything about it.'

Schafer frowned.

'Are you in some sort of trouble?' he asked quietly.

'Trouble?' Stack asked. 'No. Why, should I be?'

Schafer shrugged. 'You aren't the type to go falling over yourself.'

'I must have had too much to drink,' Stack said evasively. 'What gives?' he added.

'They're winding up the conference in East Berlin tomorrow. Press conference at two in the afternoon.'

'Conference?'

Schafer smiled patiently.

'We've been covering it together for the past two weeks,' he said. 'The East Germans have got their Warsaw friends together. All to do with Honecker's move to get full sovereign recognition. The usual propaganda charade.'

So he and Max had been covering a conference in East Berlin, Stack thought. That was what he had been doing before flying to Spain. He had been going into East Berlin. To meetings with Gunter? he wondered.

'First team on display?' he asked.

Schafer shook his head. 'Negative,' he said. 'It's their reserves, but still some of their big guns.'

'Why did you send me to Spain, Max?' Stack asked.

Schafer pulled at his cigar.

'We both thought that a change would do you good,' he replied. 'Carlos is short staffed in Madrid. It seemed a good idea at the time.'

'What do you mean, a change would do me good?'

'Ah! Come on, John,' Schafer drawled. 'You know what you've been like recently, what with Sue and...'

'What's Sue got to do with it?' Stack intervened.

'Well, I don't want to get too personal, John, but I don't think you have been the same guy since the pair of you separated. Come on, let's have another drink. I've got to see Hendrich soon.'

Schafer ordered a couple of doubles. Stack stood frowning. He wanted to know more about himself. More about the last few weeks.

'Max,' he said cautiously, 'I've got a blank, remember, about the last couple of weeks or so. You said you thought a change would do me good. Have I been irritable and awkward?'

'Hell, no,' Schafer replied. 'You haven't gone around like a bear with a sore head either, if that's what you mean.'

'But what?'

'Well, you've been quiet and unsociable, and there was that business with Hendrich Lieffer.'

'What business?'

'You seemed to have a bee in your bonnet about that article you are working on. You were looking for some organisation or something connected with refugees. You thought Lieffer could help you.'

'And he didn't,' Stack said, more to himself than Schafer. He vaguely remembered talking to Lieffer. Lieffer was in charge of the refugee office in Berlin. He should have known about the organisation, Stack thought. If anyone, Lieffer should have known.

'No, he didn't,' Schafer agreed. 'I think you thought he was holding back on you.'

'Anything else got you worried?' Stack asked. 'Let's have it, Max. Let's clear the air.'

Schafer toyed with his glass for a moment. 'All right, John, I'll give it to you straight,' he said seriously. 'You came back last December, from Prague, and you came back a different guy. Oh, you do your job okay. I've no complaints, but you don't quite tick the same. You're more distant. You are not the same guy I used to know.' He looked apologetic. 'Sorry, John, if I spoke out of turn.'

'And what have you diagnosed as the cause?' Stack asked. He knew his own problem. He wanted to know how much of it had got through to Schafer.

'You and Sue parted company last November,' Schafer replied. 'I don't know why the hell you don't make it up. A man has to be married to something, or somebody. Everybody needs something to turn them on.'

Married to something or somebody, Stack thought! My God! Stack was married all right, but not to a woman. If only he could release the spring that kept him wound up. If only he was finished with the job. He inwardly sighed. Schafer's remarks weren't anything new. He had said them before. He had even said them at Stack's wedding. A man has to be married to something, or somebody. With Stack it had been Sue – with Schafer it was his job.

'And with you it is the news business,' Stack said into his glass. 'Perhaps it is also with me.'

'Perhaps,' Schafer replied. 'But I remember how you were with Sue before the split.'

He put his arm affectionately around Stack's shoulders.

'Perhaps I am talking out of turn,' he said, 'but I see Sue, occasionally, when I go to Ruddi's studio. She does a good job for Ruddi. He is very pleased with her, but she misses you, John. I can tell.'

Stack grunted and played with his drink. His feelings for Sue seemed to be on ice, just as his feelings for everything else were in cold storage. He had taken on a job and he had fouled it up. Until he was through with it, the ice wouldn't melt. He had almost become a recluse, he knew that, but he had thought that it was safer that way.

'Tell me about this job we were covering,' he said, pointedly changing the subject.

'The East Germans called their Warsaw Pact friends together a couple of weeks ago.'

'Before that we worked on the Common Market issue?'

'You remember that?'

'Yes. It's the conference that is a blank.'

'We covered it together almost every day. I tried to get a few shots of the big names, but they wouldn't play ball. Tomorrow is the finish.'

'Any ideas?'

'Some. Honecker wants a big vote of confidence. He has been pushed into further negotiations with the West German Government by the Russians. He wants to show the West that he has the support of his allies.'

'Anything else?'

Schafer shrugged. 'Nothing that has come to light,' he said. 'Look, John, if you would rather not go, I'll send someone else.'

Stack played with his glass. He could duck out of it if he wanted to, he had the excuse, or he could take it on again. He could go back into East Berlin, he thought. Back behind the Wall. He grunted and took a long drink. As a foreign correspondent, he would have certain protection, he thought. He would be reasonably safe, but it would mean that the opposition would have their sights well and truly on him, and their finger on the trigger. It would be playing with fire. It could prove dangerous, but if he wanted his memory back he had to go over the old ground. It was his only hope.

'I'll go,' he said firmly. He had to go, he thought. He had to take the risk. He had to go where he had been meeting Gunter. He had to try and get up to date.

'I would go myself,' Schafer explained, 'but there is a briefing conference in the City Hall for Tito's visit.'

'It's being played up big,' Stack remarked.

'*De luxe* treatment,' Schafer agreed.

'When does he arrive?'

'Bonn next Tuesday and Berlin on the Wednesday. I think I might commission Ruddi to take some shots. What do you think?'

'Sure,' Stack said reluctantly. 'Why not?' He didn't like Ruddi as a person and Schafer knew it, but Ruddi was a good photographer and they often used him. Schafer and Ruddi were friendly. They were both interested in photography. Stack's resentment of Ruddi was because of Sue. She worked for Ruddi. Schafer had got her the job.

'There will be plenty of scope,' Stack added, more readily.

'Yeah,' Schafer agreed. 'Going to be an interesting visit. If we get the right shots, they could go over big in the States. They like that sort of stuff.' He looked at his watch. 'Say, John, you'll have to excuse me. I gotta meet Hendrich.'

'That's okay, Max,' Stack replied. 'By the way, would you ask Hendrich if I may call and see him tomorrow morning?'

'Sure,' Schafer replied, 'but what's on? Are you chasing up that old line of yours?'

'No,' Stack lied. 'I just want to go over some old ground to see if I can get those last few weeks back.'

'Yeah, a good idea,' Schafer said. He slapped Stack affectionately on the shoulder. 'See you tomorrow,' he said, and left the bar.

Stack stayed for one further drink to take in the faces. It was about time the opposition, or the organisation, were taking part in the game, he thought, and he wanted to flush them out before they made their move. He liked to know what was happening.

When he left the bar he followed a standard evasive pattern of movement, designed to throw up any tail. By the time he reached the vicinity of his hotel he had two suspects. One he took to be his cover, the other still had a question mark about him. He needed more time to pin him down, but he didn't get it. A large black Mercedes limousine suddenly pulled up alongside him, and two heavily built men confronted him. They were dressed in similar garb and both had a dead-pan expression on their faces that marked them as police. Stack tried to side-step them, but they blocked his way.

'Herr Stack?' one asked

'Who are you?' Stack replied.

'Police,' one said, and some form of identification flashed in front of Stack and then disappeared inside the man's jacket.

'Come with us, please.'

'Where to?' Stack asked angrily.

'Police Headquarters.'

'What for?'

'Lieutenant Keller would like to ask you a few questions,' the man said patiently.

Lieutenant Keller! Stack knew the name. Keller was in the Special Branch of the *Kriminalpolitzei*.

'Let me see your identification again,' Stack demanded. He was playing for time. He wanted his cover to see what was happening.

The man produced his identification again.

'Satisfied?' he asked grimly.

A hand touched Stack's arm, and he felt himself being crowded into the police car. Stack couldn't see his cover and silently cursed the man. He didn't question the two policemen. They wouldn't know what it was all about.

At the Police Headquarters, Stack was taken to a first-floor waiting room outside an office where the name Lt Otto Keller was printed on the door. One of Keller's men remained with him. Stack hoped like hell that his cover was using the hot line. The last thing he wanted at this stage was to get entangled with the *Kriminalpolitzei*. The minutes slowly passed by. The delay gave Stack hope. Finally, he was called into Keller's office.

Keller sat, shirt sleeved, at a desk. His hair was cut short in traditional Prussian style. He was broadly built with a stern, tanned face. He looked typical of the modern, successful German – efficient, prosperous, confident. He offered Stack a seat. His attitude gave Stack hope. He sat facing Keller.

'I am Lieutenant Keller,' Keller said formally, and sat back. 'You are John Stack?'

'I am,' Stack replied. 'And I am a British citizen,' he added. 'Employed by the European Press Agency.'

'So I understand,' Keller said. He looked at Stack. 'It would appear that you have attracted the attention of the Spanish and French police,' he added quietly.

Stack didn't reply. He decided to let Keller make all the play.

'However,' Keller added, 'before we take up the matter officially, we require further information.'

So Control had got through, Stack thought, and felt a surge of relief.

'You are free to go, Herr Stack,' Keller said slowly and guardedly, 'but you are not to leave Berlin.'

Keller stood up from his desk. So did Stack.

'It would be as well to be cautious,' Keller said seriously.

'Thank you for your advice, Herr Keller,' Stack replied.

'And I will want to talk again,' Keller added pointedly, 'when we have made further enquiries. *Auf wiedersehen,* Herr Stack.'

'*Auf wiedersehen.*'

Stack was escorted out of the building. At least he had got the police off his back, he thought. That was one less worry, and it was comforting to know that Control were still concerned about him. He picked up a taxi and returned discreetly to his hotel. In the hotel foyer, he was greeted by the receptionist with the news that Fraulein Rosier had telephoned a message to the effect that she would be late in returning. He was also told that there was a lady waiting to see him in the lounge bar.

Curiously he went into the bar and saw Sue straight away. She took him completely by surprise. She was the last person he had expected to see. He felt some of the ice inside of him crack. She looked so damned attractive. Her face had the type of classical features that were used to cover glossy magazines – high cheek bones, wide, dark eyes and a smile that toothpaste advertisers paid highly to use. Her titian hair was long and casual, and she always dressed smartly. It was a necessary part of her line of business. He got over his initial shock and frowned. She was the last, and first, person that he wanted to see. He wanted to forget her, or have her to himself. He didn't want any half measures.

She saw him and flashed a smile at him. He glanced around the other faces in the bar and they registered in his computer.

He went over to her.

'Hullo, John,' she said quietly.

Again the ice cracked. He liked the way that she dressed. Her costume was light beige and neat. It gripped her body and showed the right amount of cleavage. Just as it showed the right amount of knee and thigh. And she always wore the type of nylons that he liked. The type that had no frills or gimmicks. The plain, expensive, classy type.

'Hullo, Sue,' he said. 'Long time no see. How are you?'

'Very well, John. I'm under contract to Ruddi for the season, thanks to Max.'

'So I've heard. He's been keeping you busy. I've seen the magazines.'

The waiter came up to them.

'Same drink?' Stack asked.

'I haven't changed,' she smiled. 'You always said I was too conservative.'

'Another Martini,' he told the waiter, 'and a double whisky with water.'

Stack's surprise at seeing his wife passed. He became curious to know what had brought her.

'I heard you were in some sort of trouble,' she said, forestalling him.

'Nothing I can't handle,' Stack said evasively.

'Want to talk about it?'

'No,' Stack replied, rather harshly.

'Always the same solid John,' Sue said sadly. 'The quiet Englishman. Keep it to yourself.'

Sue was German, born and bred, despite

her English-sounding name. That was a throwback from some distant English relative. But she was also international in outlook. She had lived in England as well as Germany, and it had been in London that she and Stack had met. She had been on a modelling commission. They also generally conversed in English.

'I had an accident,' Stack explained briefly. 'I have a short lapse of memory. Nothing else.' He shrugged it off.

'I was rather worried in case you were on that plane that crashed.'

'How did you know I had gone to Spain?'

'I saw Max in Ruddi's studio one night. He told me you were going to Spain.' She offered Stack a cigarette from a packet lying on the counter. He hesitated before accepting it. He hadn't smoked a cigarette since his accident, he thought, but he was a smoker. There was his cigarette case to prove it. She produced a miniature camera. Stack looked at it. 'It is a cigarette lighter,' she smiled. 'Ruddi gave it to me. He is very good at making things. He used to be an instrument maker before he took up photography.' She pressed the lighter and a flame shot out.

'Very neat,' Stack remarked, but he wasn't interested in Ruddi. Ruddi belonged to Sue's other world. A world of high-tension advertising and artistic temperaments. Stack knew little about it, but what he did know didn't appeal.

'And how did you find me?' he asked.

'Oh! There was a message at the apartment.'

'Message?' Stack asked curiously.

'Someone telephoned about seven, to say that you were staying here. I took it to be from Max.'

'Why Max?'

'Well, he knew I was concerned about you.'

'Was it Max?'

Sue frowned. 'I don't really know,' she said. 'My cleaning woman left the message on a note pad. I just assumed that it was from Max.' She shrugged. 'Any rate, I came around.'

Stack found the cigarette distasteful and put it out. Somebody had telephoned Sue to give her his whereabouts, he thought. Why? He became suspicious. He hadn't seen his wife for several months. They had mutually kept out of each other's way.

'Why did you come?' he asked firmly.

'Well, thanks for being so pleased,' Sue replied.

'Please tell me, why?'

'I assumed you were in some sort of trouble when your whereabouts were phoned to me,' Sue said, frowning.

Phoned! Lehna was supposed to have telephoned to say that she was going to be late,

Stack thought. Someone had also telephoned Sue. Somebody was using them both. There was a trap somewhere.

'Finish your drink,' he ordered.

'Why?' Sue asked, surprised at his tone.

'I'm taking you home.'

'Well, thanks. I can see you haven't changed.'

Stack wasn't concerned about her feelings. He wanted her out of the way. There was a catch somewhere. The whole business stank to high heaven.

'Come along.'

'No dinner?' Sue asked appealingly.

'Look, Sue, I don't like you getting telephone calls about me. It's not usual. Let me take you to your flat.'

'Just what sort of trouble are you in?' she asked indignantly.

Stack sighed. He was going to have to tell her something.

'Well, the Spanish and French police would both like to have a long talk with me, to begin with,' he said lightly.

'Oh!'

'I'll tell you all about it some day when the divorce comes through.'

'You've heard from my lawyer?'

'I've heard. Come on.'

He got the receptionist to order a taxi. When it arrived, he hurried Sue out of the hotel and got into the taxi beside her. He gave the driver her address and took a quick look in the shadows near the hotel entrance. He saw no one, and wondered where his cover had gone.

The driver drove quickly.

'Well, it has been nice seeing you again,' Sue said. 'Even if I am being pushed off home in a hurry.'

'And you,' Stack grunted, but he had other things on his mind. Such as the fact that the driver wasn't taking the route that he had expected, and that there was no cover following them. His cover had lost their trail.

They turned into an area of few street lights. Stack became concerned. The driver swung into an alley and Stack got all the danger signals. Sue also sensed that something was wrong.

'Where are we going?' she asked anxiously.

The taxi stopped, abruptly, and the passenger doors flung open. Two large, burly figures appeared. Both had revolvers in their hands.

'Out!' one ordered.

Sue gave a stifled cry. Stack took her hand. She was trembling. Stack cursed himself for his stupidity. By himself he would have made a stand. With Sue, he was their prisoner. His only hope was that the men were organisation men and not the opposition. He helped Sue out of the car. Three figures surrounded them. The driver had joined his friends. Their faces were blurred lumps of flesh in the darkness. Stack looked around. At both ends of the lane was the open roadway. If only they could make a break for it, he thought desperately. A hand roughly grabbed him. It parted him from Sue. Sue screamed. Stack struggled to free himself and a fist crashed into his face. His head swam, his mouth bled. He was pushed against the wall. He heard Sue give another stifled scream as a hand covered her mouth. Stack started to fight. Furiously he lashed out. His fist connected with soft flesh, then he felt the agony of a series of blows to his body. They sank into his abdomen and kidneys. He crumpled under the pain. But he wasn't allowed the relief of collapsing to the ground. He was lifted up, and his head pressed back against the wall. It was held there until he could breathe more evenly. But the pain to his body remained. A sudden flash of metal appeared before his eyes. It was a steel blade! He felt his knees go weak. He knew what their gambit was going to be. He knew now why Sue had been tricked into visiting him. Her body was also pinned to the wall. He could feel her next to him and sensed her fear. Again the knife flashed in front of him. He struggled helplessly.

'Talk!' a voice hissed.

Stack's brain worked overtime.

'About what?' he half mumbled, his throat

dry, his body weak.

'Berak and Gunter,' the voice said.

They were opposition, Stack thought. Oh! God! They were opposition. They meant business.

'I can't remember,' he said.

Again the knife flashed in front of him. It must have touched Sue. He felt her struggle, desperately.

'I had an accident in Spain,' he said hurriedly.

'Go on.'

'Somebody attacked me,' he said. 'I am still suffering from loss of memory. For God's sake, you have to believe me. I am telling the truth – you must believe me. Don't harm her. She knows nothing.'

'What did Berak tell you?'

'I don't know what you mean.'

A hand viciously slapped his face and grabbed his clothing.

'You know!' a voice hissed.

'I don't know anything,' Stack mumbled. He couldn't talk. No matter what they did to him, or Sue, he couldn't talk. He prayed to God to let Sue faint; to pass out. What kept her going?

The knife appeared in front of him again. Sue gave a sharp, piercing scream. Stack closed his eyes. They had touched her. The bastards had marked her! He struggled furiously. His head was banged against the

103

wall. He felt the pain and his eyes momentarily lost their vision.

'Talk!' the voice ordered. 'Talk!'

No! Stack's brain shrieked at him. No! You
can't talk. You can't. No matter what they
do to Sue, you mustn't talk.

'Such a pretty face,' a voice said, and Sue
screamed again.

Stack's throat went dry. They were going to
mark her, he thought, they were… Suddenly
the area was brightly illuminated. In a flash,
the inky blackness had suddenly become
transformed, as if by magic, into a bright,
yellow light. Momentarily everything came
to a standstill, as genuine surprise took over.
From the sinister and grotesque, the figures
became normal human beings. Stack gave a
silent prayer of thanks. He saw the three
figures around them. They were big, heavy
thugs. Not the opposition's first team. Their
faces had the usual features – eyes, noses,
mouths. Stack saw them vaguely – the bald
head, the heavy growth, the grim, sadistic,
callous faces. He wouldn't forget them, not
one of them. He saw Sue beside him. Her
hair and clothing were dishevelled.

The immediate surprise passed. There was
a smack against the wall and a crack and
whine of a revolver bullet. It generated
action. The three attackers panicked. A yell,
a shout, and they let go. They got into their
taxi and shot forward, along the narrow

roadway. The lights went out and there was blackness again. Stack and Sue were alone.

Stack stopped himself from collapsing and turned to Sue. She fell into his arms and broke down, sobbing.

Stack's inside turned cold and hard. He would see this one through and he would get the person responsible. They were hitting below the belt. They were playing it dirty.

Gradually Sue's sobbing became more controllable. Stack held her close and smelled the sweet perfume of her hair. It helped to take his thoughts away from his own aches and pains. The lights that had saved them had come from the headlamps of a car, he thought. Whose car, he didn't know, and he wasn't going to find out. It had disappeared as the opposition had taken flight. It had saved them and vanished. He staggered away from the lane, helping Sue. She clung to him and they walked with difficulty. In the light from a shop window he examined her face. The knife cut was about half an inch long and close to her ear. Fortunately it was superficial and would soon heal. But she was still suffering from shock. He found another taxi and took her to her apartment, where he called in her sister who lived in the same block. After Sue had been given a sedative, he started to worry about himself. One of his ribs felt as if it had parted company from the rest of the group. The lower part of his body ached and throbbed, and a missing tooth was just a reminder that his face didn't look too good. Inga, Sue's sister, looked after him after putting Sue to bed.

'Want to tell me about it?' she asked patiently.

'Look after Sue,' Stack replied evasively.

Inga shrugged. She was older than her sister. Older and wiser. She remembered the bad times and it made her less curious.

'Why don't you stay?' she asked.

'I might one day,' Stack replied. 'In the meantime, will you take care of her?'

'Sure. I had better stay with her for a couple of days. How about you?'

'I'm a big boy now.'

'They must have been bigger by the look of things.'

'Not bigger,' Stack corrected her. 'Just more of them.'

He left Sue in the care of her sister. She was in good hands.

5

Stack stood outside the entrance to Sue's apartment block, in the shadow of the projecting canopy. Somebody knew about Sue, he thought, and was prepared to use her for their own ends. It had been a crude, unsophisticated attempt to blackmail him into talking. It showed the extent of their methods, and of their desperation. He must know something of importance. He had got over that shock, but the knowledge that they had dug into his past still disturbed him. Sue didn't belong to his business. She belonged to the glossy magazines and photographic studios. To drag her into the game made him boil up inside. Which was precisely what they wanted to do – and he knew it. He sighed, and studied the scenery, looking for any danger signs. The street was in darkness, but there was movement, and there were cars parked along the pavement. One moved away. Two men walked by, deep in conversation. He watched them. Cars approached from both directions. Opposite, was a large block of apartments. They could be watching him from inside the building, he thought. They could pick him off with a good marksman, but they wouldn't do that. Not until they knew what was inside his mind.

He stepped out from the darkness and walked toward Lyna Strasse to pick up another taxi. Ahead of him he saw the door of a parked car open. No one got out. It was the driver's door that had opened, but the driver was hidden in the darkness. What was it going to be? Stack wondered. A shot? An invitation? Or a quick hustle into the saloon? He could stop, turn, or run, he thought. Or he could be curious. His brain recalled the lights of the saloon car that had saved him and Sue. It also told him that the door had opened prematurely, probably to warn him. To put him on his guard. He walked slowly, but purposely. There were no bystanders – no pedestrians.

'Herr Stack,' a voice called out to him from inside the car. It was a gruff, quiet voice. It hadn't shouted or whispered. 'Stern Club – Schutsen Strasse, Spandau,' it said.

The door closed the car glided away from the kerb. The message got home, and so did the registration number of the car. Stack increased his pace. The organisation had made contact. It was soon going to be time for Stack to make his own personal contact. To inform Control of what he was up to.

He picked up a taxi and went into the Spandau district, but he didn't go direct to the bar. First he wanted to pull himself together, physically, and then he wanted to make sure that the opposition weren't still around. He took his time about both. The thugs in the lane had done a good job of work on him, and he didn't want a second-house performance. When he later arrived at the Stern Club he didn't feel physically on top of the world, but he was at least satisfied that there was no one tailing him. He was on his own again.

The manager of the club greeted him politely.

'You are not a member,' he said.

'I was asked to meet someone here,' Stack replied.

'Herr Stack?'

'Yes.'

The manager smiled. 'Come this way.'

Stack followed the man through a plush, thickly carpeted reception lounge into the main body of the club. The room was crowded with people; the tables jammed close together. The atmosphere was colour-ful, noisy, and off beat, and so were many of the customers. On a small, brilliantly lit stage two nude coloured girls were performing an unusual ritual fertility dance that seemed to delight the audience.

Stack was taken to a corner table hidden in a recess, where a man sat alone. The man stood up. The manager bowed politely and left them.

The two men confronted each other. Facing Stack was a man of medium height, smartly dressed in a dark suit with a conservative taste in shirt and tie. He looked much older than Stack. His dark eyes held Stack firmly in their gaze. His face was round, his hair fine, almost balding. It was a face that was neither handsome nor ugly, despite a number of pock-marked scars on the chin. It was the type of face that looked as if it had emerged through a jungle of battles and trouble, to a new type of wealth. It looked as if it reflected the history of Berlin itself.

'Herr Stack,' the man said in a gruff, Berlin accent. He held out his hand. It was a small, podgy hand, but with a firm handshake. The man indicated the vacant chair opposite him. Stack sat down.

'You have the advantage over me,' Stack said.

The man gave a faint smile.

'Call me Schmidt,' he said, 'for convenience.' He produced a cigar case, offered a cigar to Stack, who refused, and lit his own cigar. A waiter appeared.

'What will you drink?' Schmidt asked.

'Beer,' Stack replied.

Schmidt ordered two steins.

'I represent a travel organisation, Herr Stack,' Schmidt said quietly. 'You understand?'

110

'I understand,' Stack replied.

The waiter brought their drinks.

'*Prosit,*' Schmidt said.

Stack returned the salute.

'How is your wife?' Schmidt asked, slowly placing his stein on the table.

Stack looked directly into the man's eyes.

'What wife?' he asked.

Schmidt smiled patiently. 'Please,' he said. 'I have done my homework.'

Stack didn't reply.

'What happened to your wife tonight was crude and stupid,' Schmidt said airily.

'I am grateful to you for your help,' Stack said.

'I shouldn't be too grateful. I think my arrival was welcomed by both parties. Unless, of course, you were going to talk.'

'There was nothing to talk about,' Stack said gruffly.

'Are you a British agent, Herr Stack?' Schmidt asked calmly, changing the subject.

'No,' Stack replied, equally calmly.

Schmidt raised his eyebrows.

'Then you have problems,' he said. 'You and your wife are attacked, very crudely, by three men. Why? You say you are not a British agent, but the three men are well known for their allegiance to the Communist camp.'

'I have no idea why I was attacked,' Stack replied frankly. 'I have no idea why I was also attacked in Spain. I don't doubt that you know that as well.'

'I know.'

'Then you will also know that a certain doctor got me out of Spain and asked me for help in obtaining a package from the East.'

'I know,' Schmidt said again.

'My companion needs the help of your organisation,' Stack said grimly. 'That is as far as my interest is concerned. If we don't do business, it will not upset me.'

'But it will upset Fraulein Rosier.'

'It will,' Stack agreed, 'but I am not sure that I care.'

'But she has already paid for a ticket,' Schmidt said, with a look of feigned concern.

'Just how reliable is your travel agency?' Stack asked. He was thinking of Berak. Berak had also paid for his ticket, and Berak was dead.

Schmidt shrugged.

'Everything is relative,' he said in an off-hand manner. 'Your package will be travelling on a third-class ticket. That is more dangerous than if it was travelling first-class.'

'How much would a first-class ticket cost?'

Schmidt played with his cigar.

'What those three men were after,' he said quietly.

'No dice,' Stack said emphatically. 'We stick to our original deal, or not at all.'

Schmidt opened his hands in a gesture of 'so be it'.

'The package is a man called Criller?' he asked.

'Yes. Paul Criller. Age, twenty-six years. A man of slim build, dark hair. Wears glasses. From Leipzig.'

'And his present location?'

Stack shrugged. 'Unfortunately, I don't know exactly.'

'You must, if you want to pass on his instructions.'

They looked at each other.

'I'll find out,' Stack said. 'How do I contact you?'

'We'll contact you. What are your movements tomorrow?'

Stack told him.

'Go to the Opera Café next door to the State Opera, in Unter den Linden Strasse, in East Berlin,' Schmidt ordered. 'It is close to the border. Sit at the third table from the extreme left in the second row, facing the road. The waiter's name is Alfonso. The table will have a reserved sign. The waiter will ask you to move. Order an English tea. We will leave Criller's instructions on the back of the ticket that you will receive from the waiter.'

Schmidt finished off his beer. Their

113

meeting was at an end. They both stood up and shook hands.

'Good night, Herr Stack,' Schmidt said. *'Auf wiedersehen.'*

As Stack left the club, he wondered how much trust and loyalty he could expect from Schmidt and his organisation. Berak hadn't got any. Would Criller get any more? He was still thinking about Schmidt when he reached his hotel. He found that Lehna had returned and was in her room. He ordered a double Scotch, sank it, and went to see her.

She was pleased to see him, but there was a look on her face that suggested something had gone wrong. He thought how different she was from Sue. Sue was titian, glamorous, dress conscious and sexy, and knew how to look after a man. Lehna was dark, with an expressive face, and an Eastern air of mystery about her. She also had sex, but her sex was quieter and she didn't play with it like Sue. It was almost accidental. She sat on the bed with her robe wrapped around her. There was no leg show.

Stack flopped into a chair. He suddenly felt very tired. His body still ached. He wanted rest, but first he knew that he had to clear the air with Lehna. There was that look on her face – the hurt, sad look.

'It's been one hell of a night,' he sighed.

'Want to tell me about it?'

'Sure.'

He told her, but played down the rough stuff.

'I didn't telephone any message to you,' Lehna frowned when he had finished, 'but it explains something suspicious.'

'What?' Stack asked.

'My taxi broke down on the return journey. We were held up for some time.'

Stack wasn't surprised. The whole evening had been engineered to suit someone's purpose. Someone other than Lehna, Sue, or Stack.

'You saw Franz Hessler?'

Lehna's face clouded over. She had looked sullen from the moment Stack had joined her. He had put it down to a pique of temper at being kept waiting. Now he learned otherwise, and he immediately forgot about his ego.

'Franz Hessler is dead,' she said sadly. 'He had an accident two days ago.'

'Accident?' Stack asked suspiciously.

'Stepped off the pavement and was hit by a passing truck.'

'I'm sorry,' Stack said earnestly, and wondered if Hessler's accident could have been carefully planned. He had no grounds for suspicion, but untimely accidents always troubled him. 'So you don't have Paul's address in the Eastern Zone?' he asked.

'I know where he can be contacted,' she sighed. 'It is through Frau Schoneberg. She runs a coffee stall in the Ice Stadium in Zieten Strasse, in East Berlin. Can we get a message to him?'

'There are ways and means,' Stack said. 'Did Hessler leave any close relatives?'

'No,' Lehna replied. 'He lived alone. His housekeeper let me into his room. She remembered my name from the back of the envelopes that I sent to him.'

Something made Stack suspicious. He felt there was more to come.

'What did you find?'

'Nothing really,' she shrugged, 'except a few photographs.'

She opened her handbag and produced a number of post-card type pictures.

'Let me see them,' Stack asked.

She handed them to him. Several were of an elderly, grey-haired woman. None of them meant anything to Stack – except one. It was a photograph of a man and a woman talking to each other. Stack's inside went numb.

'Who did Hessler work for?' he asked with surprised calmness.

'The Europa Photographic Studios,' Lehna said. 'He was in charge of the processing department. He was also an expert photographer himself. Do you recognise the man or woman?'

'Yes,' Stack said flatly. 'The man is Rudolph Schooner, better known as Ruddi. He is the

director of the agency.'
  'And the woman?'
  'My wife!'

6

The following morning Stack was up and about very early. He still felt stiff and bruised from the rough handling he had received the previous evening, but he also felt a pre-match type of excitement. It was all happening. He could sense it. The sudden pattern of events was bringing the issue to life. Hessler had worked for Ruddi. So did Sue, and Sue had been brought into the play. Somebody knew about Stack's movements at the time of Berak's escape. Somebody had tipped off the Communists. That somebody had to be close to Stack. Stack's memory still hadn't given up all its facts, but some had come back. He remembered visiting Sue at Ruddi's studio to sort out some legal matter. There could be a tie-up through Sue somewhere. It was a possible line of investigation. There was also Max, who knew more about Stack than anyone else. And there was Hendrich Lieffer. But it was no good trying to play detective, he thought. His intuition told him that there wasn't time. It also told him to let them make the play. They had so far. What he had to do was to go along with it until he got his memory back, but he had to take precautions. It was time to inform his Control what was going on.

He went to his apartment in Kurfiersten Strasse and prepared a carefully worded message. It gave a complete résumé of his movements since he had flown to Spain. It also asked Control to get information on the contacts he had made. He photographed the coded message and placed the micro film in a metal sachet the size of a small postage stamp. This was stapled to the corner of a ten mark note. A note which was later used to buy a morning newspaper from the stand outside the Ernst Reuter underground station – Stack's main post box to his Control.

After preparing his message, he returned to his hotel for breakfast. Lehna joined him.

'I would like to come with you today,' she said eagerly. 'The last thing I want to do is sit about, and I don't care if there is a risk. I have an Israeli passport.'

Stack shook his head.

'Sorry,' he said. 'I don't think that would be wise.'

He was going to be out in the open, he thought. Everything he did now could be observed and reported back to the opposition. He was even going into their territory. But there was no need to take Lehna into the front line. He wanted to protect her as much as possible. He shook his head. 'Sorry,' he said again. She looked crestfallen.

'When will I see you?' she asked.

'Lunch time,' he replied cheerfully. 'I know a nice restaurant where we can have lunch. I'll meet you at one o'clock.'

He gave her the name and address of the restaurant, and suggested that she remained in the hotel during the morning, where she was safe. She smiled faintly at his suggestion, and made no comment.

Stack left her after breakfast and took the underground to Ernst Reuter Strasse. He didn't bother to concern himself about a tail. He took it that someone would be there, and so long as he was being legitimate, they were harmless. At the newsagent shop in the station, he purchased a British newspaper and made his pass. At the office, the staff greeted him warmly and made one or two wisecracks about his lost memory. It was a close-knit unit that worked well. An ideal cover for his other activities.

He telephoned Sue and learned that she was still resting, but that she had recovered from her shock. He felt relieved. His blood still boiled at the thought of the way she had been manhandled the previous evening. He got a promise out of Sue's sister that she would stay close to her, and rang off. He put her to the back of his mind, and studied the reports and papers on his desk. He found the draft of the article he had been working on about the refugee problem and read it eagerly, but it was an economical, and statistical, study, rather than an investigation into escape organisations. It gave him no lead whatsoever as to the identity of Schmidt or his organisation. Without Lorenzo's help, he would have still been in the dark.

As he was studying the draft, Max Schafer arrived at the office. He looked as if he had had a rough night. He called Stack into his office.

'I thought you were dining with Lieffer last night?' Stack remarked.

'I did,' Schafer replied. 'He took me to the Town Hall to get the inside on the arrangements for the State Visit next Wednesday.'

'Did that take all night?'

'Hell, no, but I met a guy from the West German Foreign Department. He was very interesting. We had a session at Hendrich's place and then went to a club.'

'Any news?'

'They're putting a lot of stock on Tito's visit,' Schafer commented. 'It will be another feather in their cap.'

Which the Communists wouldn't like, Stack thought.

'You okay?' Schafer asked. 'How's the memory?'

'Still the blanks,' Stack replied, 'but I'm okay. Did you ask Lieffer if he would see me?'

'Yeah,' Schafer replied, and looked at his watch. 'He'll see you in fifteen minutes' time, precisely.'

'Thanks. By the way, Max. Did you telephone Sue yesterday?'

'Sue?' Schafer asked. 'No. Was I supposed to?'

'No,' Stack replied. 'Forget it.'

Schafer shrugged.

'Anything else?' Stack asked.'

'Got a cable from New York,' Schafer said. 'They'll take all the shots I can get of the state visit.'

'Paying well?'

'Top rate. Pity we couldn't get any of that conference in East Berlin.'

Schafer's telephone rang. He picked it up. 'See you when you get back,' he called to Stack.

'Okay, Max.'

Stack left Schafer's office and collected the necessary papers and documents from the office manager. He was an accredited representative of the Press Agency again, and as such he would be reasonably safe in East Berlin. They wouldn't touch him whilst he was on official business. Not unless they were desperate, and if their information source was as effective as Stack imagined, they would now be aware that he was suffering from a memory lapse, and was therefore harmless.

He took one of the agency cars and drove direct to Lieffer's office. He hoped his visit would unlock another door of his mind. He felt Lieffer had a key, but he also felt that Lieffer wouldn't want to use it. There was something about Hendrich Lieffer that made Stack cautious. Lieffer was the dynamic type of business man of the new German reformation. What the modern buildings and affluent society had developed from the ruins of 1945, men like Lieffer had emerged to lead the new régime. He was an assistant director of the Ministry of Refugees, in charge of the Berlin office. A Ministry whose documentation and information were valuable to many bodies and activities. Stack respected Lieffer, but there the relationship ended. Lieffer was much older than Stack. Older, wealthier, and with a patronising air that rankled Stack, and he had shown an unhealthy interest in Stack's activities.

Lieffer's outer office gave the correct impression. It was functional in design and busy in appearance. Stack was taken to a waiting-room in which figures and graphs were displayed on the wall, indicating both the enormity of the refugee problem and the Ministry's thoroughness in statistical records. Fortunately for Stack, Lieffer's personal secretary soon released him from his study of the information and took him to Lieffer's office. Lieffer was at his desk, but stood up as Stack entered the room. He was of similar height to Stack, and immaculately dressed in a dark suit. On his finger he displayed an expensive gold ring. He also wore a gold identification bracelet. His face was tanned, round and even featured; his grey hair, sleek and neat. But there was also the faintest trace that he was starting to go to seed. There was the first sign of flab about his face and figure.

They shook hands.

'Max told me that you are still recovering from a loss of memory,' Lieffer remarked, offering a gold cigar box. Stack declined to take a cigar. Lieffer closed the box.

'Yes, Herr Lieffer,' Stack agreed. 'There are still a few blank spots.'

'You remember spending a couple of hours in my department about four weeks ago?' Lieffer asked, 'and last week?'

'I remember coming to your department several weeks ago,' Stack replied, 'but not the second time.'

'Your first visit was when you asked about this organisation that interests you.'

'And you couldn't help?'

'No.'

Or wouldn't help, Stack thought.

'And the second visit, Herr Lieffer?' he asked.

'You asked to see some records.'

'And did I?' Stack asked.

'Yes,' Lieffer replied.

'Would you mind if I inspected the documents again?'

'Not at all,' Lieffer replied patiently. He threw a switch on his intercommunication set and gave instructions for Stack to be given access to their records.

Stack thanked him.

'If you would tell me what it is all about, perhaps I could be of further help to you,' Lieffer suggested.

Perhaps, Stack thought, but Lieffer hadn't helped him when he had needed help most. That was why Berak was dead.

'That is very kind of you, Herr Lieffer,' he said, 'but I'm afraid I am still in the dark myself.'

'Have you seen a doctor?' Lieffer asked.

'Yes,' Stack replied, 'in Barcelona. Perhaps you know him. His name is Lorenzo.'

Lieffer nodded his head in agreement.

'I have heard of him,' he said. 'He is well known amongst the authorities.'

'In what way?'

'He used to help refugees get to Palestine. He is a rather colourful character.'

'Yes, he is,' Stack agreed.

He stood up.

'Thank you for giving me so much of your time,' he said formally.

They shook hands.

'The mind can play tricks,' Lieffer said

quietly. 'It is well to be cautious before jumping to conclusions when the mind is in its fanciful mood.'

The two men looked at each other. Lieffer smiled.

'I am only offering advice,' Lieffer added quietly. 'You have appeared so tense these past few weeks that I worry in case you are becoming a victim of the undercurrents of mystery and secrecy that our position here in Berlin seems to have developed.'

'Thank you for your advice,' Stack replied seriously. 'I am a journalist, and the search for truth and news often misleads people into doubting our motives, but in the main we are simple folk who have a healthy desire to stick to our objectives and not become involved.'

Lieffer nodded his head approvingly.

'*Auf wiedersehen,*' he said.

'*Auf wiedersehen,*' Stack replied.

He left the director's room and was taken to the records department, where he was met by a bespectacled, elderly woman. She was as equally efficient as her image presented, as Stack found out.

'We have further particulars on the file that interested you at your last visit, Herr Stack,' she said. 'We have the report now from the border guards.'

Stack complimented her on her memory. She handed him a file. It had a coded reference and was numbered, but to Stack it was Emil Berak.

He studied the cold, clinical facts of Berak's file. The name and known history of the victim were given. Also the place, time, and date of his attempted escape. On June 9th Berak had been shot, dead, by the East German guards, near a deserted churchyard at Fenstadt. The additional information referred to by the assistant was the report of the West German border guards. At 23.00 hours, the East German searchlights had swept the area. A small, orange glow had pinpointed Berak's position. The border guard suspected that Berak had accidentally set off a small trip flare which had given away his position. He had been instantly shot at by machine gun fire and hit six times. Berak had been alone in his attempted escape. There was no other person whom Stack could consult.

Stack read the facts and returned the documents. He thanked the woman for her help, but he had found out nothing new, except for the information given in the report of the West German border guard. He had gone over old ground and still the doors of his mind remained locked. If they failed to open soon, he thought grimly, he would have also failed, because whatever his mind was keeping closed from him would soon become history. He felt the danger was that imminent.

He left Lieffer's office and took a sight-seeing trip around the city before going to the restaurant where he had arranged to meet Lehna. He still hoped to protect her from becoming involved, especially after the way Sue had been treated the previous evening.

Lehna hadn't arrived at the restaurant. Stack went to the bar and ordered a drink. He had been in Berlin almost twenty-four hours, he thought sadly, and he was getting very few of the islands of memory that Lorenzo had referred to, never mind a full recovery. If only he could remember what Berak had got on to, or what it was connected with, but he couldn't. He sighed and took a drink. The newspapers were playing up President Tito's visit. Had it anything to do with that, he wondered? Were the Communists out to spike the German Chancellor's guns? Honecker, who had taken over as the number one man in East Germany, was a disciple of the old school. He and his friends were setting up their hard line at their conference. Were they also planning to undermine Tito's visit? Was that what Berak had got on to?

Lehna arrived as Stack started his second drink. She refused a cocktail and they sat at a table. She was smartly dressed in a light-coloured suit that attracted the eye of several other customers. Stack liked it. He also liked having her around. She was emotionally uncomplicated. With her, he could relax.

'I didn't remain in the hotel,' she said guiltily, after they had ordered lunch.

'You didn't?' Stack asked, frowning.

'Don't be cross,' she said hurriedly. 'I couldn't. I wanted to do some sight-seeing.'

'Sight-seeing?' Stack asked suspiciously.

'I took a sight-seeing bus tour of East Berlin,' she said.

Stack opened his mouth to chastise her.

'I have my passport,' she explained. 'There was no risk.'

'No risk,' Stack sighed, but let it pass. 'Okay,' he said. 'You went sight-seeing. What did you see?'

She told him about her trip around the Eastern sector. She hadn't been impressed. He watched her as she talked. Her features were not particularly Jewish, he thought. She could have belonged to any of the Balkan countries. She spoke to him normally in English, but she was equally at home with other languages. He really knew very little about her, and she about him.

She smiled at him.

'What are you thinking about?' she asked.

'You.'

'Thank you.'

'Whereabouts is the Kibbutz in Israel?'

She told him. He hadn't heard of the place,

or the area, but he would remember it.

'And you were a teacher?'

'Are,' she corrected him. 'I hope to return to it, soon.'

'Yes,' Stack said. He had noticed that she had lowered her eyes and wondered why. 'And you have never been abroad before?' he asked.

She looked up at him, frowned, and looked away again.

'That's not quite true,' she said quietly. 'I have been abroad before – several times.' She played with her table napkin. 'I suppose I wanted you to think of me as some helpless innocent,' she added ruefully, 'to get you to help me.'

Stack didn't reply. He was wondering how much more there was about her that wasn't quite true.

'But I've never been to Berlin before,' she sighed, 'and I wish I had never come.'

He looked at her with surprise.

'I've done the sights,' she said. 'The Wall and East Berlin.'

'And?'

She furrowed her brow and frowned.

'Before I came here, I thought it would be all like a game. It was an adventure. Even when I met Doctor Lorenzo, and then you, it all seemed to be as I had expected.' She wasn't looking at him. 'That day at the hotel in Marseilles was great fun,' she said, and looked past him. 'Then the fun stopped with Henri Gallon,' she added sadly, 'and Berlin.'

'And Berlin?' Stack asked, encouraging her to go on.

She shook herself, as if trying to shake off some feeling.

'The whole city has an air of intrigue and mystery about it,' she said scornfully. 'Even the travel brochures play on it. Go to East Berlin, they say, and every man in a trench coat will look like a potential spy.'

'That's for the tourists,' Stack said lightly.

'Those guards on the Wall are for real,' she replied earnestly, 'and those men that attacked you last night weren't acting.' She dropped her eyes. 'I wish I had never come,' she whispered.

The waiter served their meal. Stack saw two men enter the restaurant and glance suspiciously around the tables. Lehna was correct, he thought. It was a city of mystery and intrigue.

'There is still Criller,' he pointed out.

'Paul?' Lehna looked wistful. 'Girlish dreams, perhaps.' Her face became serious. 'It is too dangerous,' she whispered. 'Those guards on the Wall brought it home to me. Paul could be killed. It is not worth it. I don't want any bloodshed on my account.'

'On your account?'

From a corner of his eye, Stack saw the

two men move to a table close to where he and Lehna were sitting.

'I persuaded Paul to try and escape,' Lehna said. 'Now I wish I hadn't. I wish I could forget all about it.'

'Can you forget about it now?'

She didn't answer. Stack caught her looking at the two men. He turned her attentions back to him.

'Can you forget about it now?' he asked again.

'Yes,' she said emphatically. 'Oh! I don't know,' she added. 'I just don't want anyone to get hurt.'

'They won't,' Stack said encouragingly, and wondered where the two men fitted into her thoughts. Had she seen them before?

'What about your wife?' Lehna asked abruptly, changing the subject.

'What about her?' Stack asked.

'How is she this morning?'

'Still resting,' Stack replied, 'but she has got over the shock. She will be at the studio this afternoon.' Ruddi's studio, he thought, and wondered if that was such a wise move for Sue. There was a tie-up somewhere.

'Are you going through with your divorce?' Lehna asked hesitantly. She dropped her eyes when she saw Stack look up with surprise.

'That depends,' Stack said. Depends on how he felt when his present business was finished, he thought. How he felt about Sue.

How she felt about him. But he didn't want to talk about it. 'It will sort itself out,' he added. 'What has to be will be.'

'You can help it along, or change its course,' Lehna said pensively. 'You can be master of your own ship.'

'Are you master of yours?' Stack asked.

Again Lehna dropped her eyes.

'No,' she said sadly. 'No. I wish I was.' She looked up and saw his puzzled look. 'Please don't ask me anything,' she pleaded. 'Please.'

'Okay.' Stack shrugged. 'Anything you say.'

'Thank you.'

She became silent. Stack wondered if it had anything to do with the two men watching them. Her attitude had changed after she had noticed them. He looked at the two men again. They didn't look like policemen, he thought, so that meant they belonged to some special organisation. Unless they were Schmidt's men.

They finished their meal and left the restaurant. Lehna seemed anxious to get back to their hotel. As they got into their car, Stack saw one of the two men from the restaurant hailing a taxi. He made certain that they lost him, quickly.

In the hotel, Lehna still remained unusually silent. When it was time for Stack to leave for the conference she mustered up a faint smile.

'Take care of yourself,' she said quietly,

with feeling.

'Sure,' Stack agreed. 'See you when I return.'

Her attitude bothered him as he drove to Friedrich Strasse. He didn't like to think of her being troubled and upset. When he drove into Checkpoint Charlie, however, he forgot about her. The Wall always had a monopolising effect on his thoughts, as did the East German guards with their automatic weapons.

The guards went through the pantomime of inspecting his documents and the car. It was a slow procedure, aimed at instilling some kind of awareness into the would-be visitor. They need not have bothered. The effect was felt as soon as the visitor entered the Eastern Sector – capital of the German Democratic Republic.

The Eastern Sector of the city differed from the Western Sector, and their differences were not only in the ideals of the two régimes, or the architecture of their buildings. There was also a difference in the very heartbeat of the city. The traffic was not so busy in the East; the shops not so decorative, and the people not so bustling.

Stack felt the differences as he continued along Friedrich Strasse. The feeling became stronger as he turned into Unter den Linden Strasse, and came to the Marx Engles Platz. The area was cordoned off with police and military. He was stopped at a control point and his credentials checked. He was allowed to pass and proceed to a car park. Other journalists were parking their cars. Some of their faces were familiar. It made him feel easier. Together, they went into the building of the Council of State.

The assembly hall where the press conference was being held displayed photographs of the grim, unyielding faces of the Communist leaders. The hall seemed to epitomize the cold, functional approach of the Communists in East Germany under Honecker's leadership. Stack had been in the room many times. The ghosts of Berak and Gunter were present. He could feel them. It had been at such gatherings that Berak had often passed his messages. Stack felt sad as he reflected on those moments. They seemed a long time ago. Gunter had also attended such meetings, he thought. How had Gunter made his pass? How had Gunter operated? Berak had been quite brazen. What about Gunter? Silently Stack racked his brains. Berak was an open book to him. Even the tense, anxious days when Berak had been arranging his defection were quite clear to him. But Gunter was a mystery. Feverishly Stack tried to slot him into the sequence of events, but they wouldn't come. He scanned the room searching for some familiar sign or object to start his memory going again. His eyes fell on a man watching him. Instantly he knew that they had met before. The man was of slim build with flaxen hair, and had a stiff, efficient air about him. Momentarily the rest of the assembled gathering didn't exist. Stack and the man eyed each other, and Stack knew where they had met. The man had been standing in the reception foyer of the Hotel Excelsior in Barcelona! The man was a Communist agent! He had probably followed Stack to Spain! Now he was openly watching him in his own parlour! Stack turned away, and he suddenly felt as if the temperature in the room had dropped. There was now a cold chill about the atmosphere.

A spokesman of the German Democratic Republic came to the front of the platform and started to read from a prepared hand-out, which the Press were to be given later. The conference, they were told, expressed, unanimously, its support of the policies of the Warsaw Pact Defence Organisation, and reiterated that the countries of the Organis-ation would not allow any interference in the internal affairs of any of their friends or allies by the United States or any other NATO government. After the expression of support, indirectly directed to the policies of the Soviet Union, came the sabre rattling. The speaker went on to compare the might of the Russian Fleet in the Mediterranean with that of the U.S. Sixth Fleet. Stack recalled some of the documents that Berak had passed to him. They had shown the concern that the Soviet Union felt at not having a suitable naval base in the Mediterranean. They had also told of an unsuccessful attempt made by the Russians to establish a base in the Balkans. The threats and warnings now coming from the platform were undoubtedly being aimed at the meeting of the West German Chancellor and the Yugoslav President. It was a clear message of warning. Yugoslavia was part of the Balkans. It was also on a razor's edge. The forthcoming state visit was not to change its status in any way.

From the international scene, the speaker referred to the current negotiations being undertaken between the German Democratic Republic and the West German Federal Government over further access rights and movement in Berlin between the two zones. The conference was united in its support of the German Democratic Government and its rightful demand for full sovereign recognition before acceding to any requests made by the West German Federal Government. There was to be no soft touch on Berlin, Stack thought. Any agreement was going to have a high price. The speech abruptly ended. The speaker had read the statement. There were to be questions.

There was a general movement of the journalists sitting in the main body of the hall. They discussed the statement amongst themselves. The essence and real purpose of the conference had been to give weight and support to Honecker in his negotiations with the Federal German Government, they thought. It was known that he had been pushed into the negotiations by the Russians. Stack wondered what else had been agreed behind the locked doors. They had made it clear that Tito was not to shuffle any closer to the West. The *status quo* had not to be changed. Had they taken any precautions to make sure that it didn't, Stack wondered? Had anything else been planned? Had Berak's contact actually passed on to Gunter what was being discussed behind their locked doors? Stack felt himself perspiring. He was on the right track, he thought. There was something familiar about that line of thought. He could feel his excitement starting to trickle through his body like the first stream after a drought. He was thinking right. It made him feel good.

The journalists started to move into the anteroom to contact their offices. Stack stood up and found he was still being closely watched. It irritated him. He purposely made sure that he passed by his watchdog. As he came up to the man, he took the initiative.

'Have we met before?' he asked.

If the man was surprised at Stack forcing the issue, he didn't show it.

'I don't think so, Herr Stack,' the man replied calmly, his eyes unflinching.

'You have the advantage over me,' Stack said. 'You know my name.'

'Heltman Preiser,' the man replied formally, and bowed his head.

'Press or police?' Stack asked.

'Like you, Herr Stack,' Preiser said cynically. 'Press.'

Stack smiled. 'You will excuse me,' he said. 'I have to make my report.' He looked directly at Preiser. 'Are you certain we didn't meet in Barcelona?' he asked. 'At the Hotel Excelsior, for instance?'

'We did not,' Preiser replied evenly, 'but I feel certain that we will meet again.'

So did Stack. Preiser was another cold fish, he thought. Cold and efficient like the man who had enlisted Stack into British Intelligence. They must be an international breed, he thought.

Preiser moved away, and Stack went into the anteroom. He got straight through to the office and dictated his copy to a typist. Within seconds it would be flashed around the world. When his copy had been accepted, he was put through to Schafer.

'What gives?' Schafer asked.

'Support for Honecker's hard line,' Stack

139

replied. 'They are also trying to kill Tito's visit before it starts. Anything at your end?'

'No,' Schafer grumbled.

'When are you flying to Bonn?' Stack asked.

'Probably tonight,' Schafer replied. 'I've got several other interested bodies lined up for a picture cover of the visit. We are on the gravy trail with this one. I'll keep in touch.'

'Okay, Max.'

Stack rang off and momentarily stood looking at the telephone. If only he could remember, he thought. If only Gunter would come back to him. There was something in the air. The mood of the conference had shown that. Berak had forecast trouble. So had British Intelligence. That was why Stack had pushed Berak to the limit. If only he could remember. But he couldn't, and he suddenly hated the whole bloody business. He turned away from the telephone stand. The room was noisy and crowded, but he saw Preiser straight away. He was standing in the corner, stone faced, taking it all in. So were his assistants, who stood by his side. Stack had had enough. To hell with them all, he thought. He left the room and hurried back to his car. He would pick up the instructions for Criller at the café, he thought, and go back to the hotel. It would be good to get back to the Western Zone again. He drove out of the car park, but was again held up at the police cordon and his documents checked. When he was cleared, he left the Platz and drove into the tree-lined Unter den Linden Strasse.

He parked the car opposite the Opera Café. Another car parked alongside him. Two men got out. Preiser's men! They weren't hiding the fact that they were tailing him. He walked, casually, over to the tables on the pavement. The two men followed. He tried to ignore them. He went to the table, as instructed. It was reserved. He sat down. An elderly waiter came up to him and looked apologetic.

'The table is reserved,' the waiter said. 'Would you mind sitting at this table?' He offered Stack another table.

Stack saw the name card on the waiter's waistcoat. He was Alfonso.

'Certainly,' Stack said. 'I would like a cup of English tea.' He sat at the table and saw that the two men had taken a table nearby.

The waiter brought the tea. Preiser's men watched. They weren't trying to hide their interest. Stack calmly drank the tea and examined the ticket. On the reverse side was written: Huster Hotel, Witten Strasse, Room 14. Collection 2 a.m. He finished his tea and walked slowly back to his car. Preiser's men followed him, and they stayed with him until he passed through the control point at Checkpoint Charlie.

7

Stack returned to the hotel as soon as he entered the Western Zone. It was now a case of getting the information to Criller, he thought, and the rest would be up to the organisation. But Stack wasn't finished with Schmidt. Once Criller was safely through the pipeline, he had plans for Schmidt.

Lehna wasn't in the hotel lounge. Nor was she in her room. Stack went to the reception desk to see if she had left a message. She hadn't, but the reception clerk had some information for him.

'Fraulein Rosier checked out of the hotel,' he explained. 'She made a reservation with Pan Am and left for the airport.'

Pan Am! Airport! Stack frowned. Lehna was leaving Berlin. She was returning to Israel. Why, he wondered? Why?

'What time was this?' he asked.

'About two-thirty, Herr Stack,' the receptionist replied.

Shortly after he had left her, Stack thought. He thanked the man and went to his room. Lehna's actions puzzled him. He didn't understand why she should leave Berlin in such a hurry when Criller was so close to achieving his goal. It just didn't make sense. He felt the frustration swell inside of him. He didn't understand what was going on. Blast! He thought. Blast!

His telephone rang. He grabbed at it eagerly. It was Sue. That also surprised him. So did her concern.

'Are you all right, John?' she asked.

'Yes,' he replied, 'but I should be asking you that.'

'I'm sorry I behaved rather childishly last night,' she said.

'Childishly! That's rubbish, Sue. Your reactions were understandable. My God, the treatment you got. Sue, I will never forgive myself for getting you involved.'

'I'm glad you did,' Sue said.

'Glad?'

'Well, I'm beginning to understand a few things now,' she said. 'That is why I rang.' There was a fractional pause. 'John,' she added quietly. 'There have been one or two suspicious things happening recently. Could we meet? I would like to talk to you about them.'

'What sort of things?' Stack asked, deeply interested.

'Oh, little things,' Sue said. 'Like the feeling of being followed.'

'Followed!'

'Yes.'

'What time can I meet you?' Stack asked

grimly. 'Are you free this evening?'

'Not until about eleven,' Sue replied. 'I have a show at the Grand Hotel for Ruddi.'

'I'll pick you up at the hotel,' Stack said. 'I'll be in the bar. We can have dinner.'

'That will be nice, John.'

Sue rang off. Stack was impressed. For weeks she had been out of his life. Now she had become involved, and she didn't seem to mind. Even the attack of the previous evening was being cast aside by her as of little consequence. Was this a new Sue, he wondered? He hoped so. Or was it another way of getting at him? He shrugged and thought of Lehna again. He wished she hadn't run out on him. Now that he had linked up with the organisation, he didn't want to foul them up. And there was Criller being left suspended. He looked thoughtfully at the telephone and decided to check on Lehna's movements a stage further. He rang Pan Am, at Tempelhof Airport, and was told that a Fraulein Rosier had booked a flight to Bonn and had checked in, but that she had not boarded the aircraft! Stack's alarm bells started ringing. Somewhere between checking in and the actual flight, Lehna had left the airport! He went to the bar and sank a double Scotch. What had happened to her, he wondered? Had she left the airport on her own account? Or had she been taken by interested parties? He felt his inside freeze up. He didn't like it. There was more to this than he knew of, and Criller was tied up in it somewhere. And it had probably nothing to do with marriage. There was something else involved. That was why Lehna had walked out on Stack. He ordered another drink. He didn't like being left hanging in mid air. He didn't like anything half-finished. He had to know what it was about. Criller, he thought! Criller could supply some of the answers, and he knew where Criller could be contacted in East Berlin. He mulled it over in his mind. There was no problem getting into East Berlin, he thought. He had a British passport and all the necessary papers. There were no restrictions on his movements. He was not subject to the controls inflicted on the West Berliners. The G.D.R. had opened its doors to tourists. There were even sightseeing trips by day and night. That was no problem. But there was Preiser. He would be on the look-out for Stack, and he would have informed all the control points. But East Berlin was a big place, Stack thought. With a car he could soon shake off any tails, and if he couldn't – well, he would just have to call it off. It was still worth a try, he thought. He gave a grunt. He had no other course open to him. He had to go.

He left the bar and telephoned a nearby garage, and arranged to have a dark Mercedes saloon brought immediately to the hotel. He also rang his office and told them that he was going into East Berlin and they could leave a message for him at the Inter Hotel. It was a secondary precaution on his part, just in case anything should go wrong.

When the car arrived, Stack drove around the area until he was satisfied that he was not being tailed. He then went to his apartment and changed his clothing and appearance as much as possible. When it turned dark he again passed through Checkpoint Charlie. Only this time there was the added feeling of knowing that he wasn't on official Press business. From the control point he drove through the city centre and into the quiet back streets. It was much easier for him to check if he was being followed in East Berlin than in the West. There was much less traffic about. Several times he stopped the car and waited to see if he was attracting attention, but there was no sign of anybody taking an interest in him. He was on his own. He drove into the vicinity of the Stadium. He was still on his own. It was as he had hoped, but nevertheless he began to feel uneasy. He parked the car where he could observe the entrance to the Stadium, and sat watching the arrivals and departures. He saw nothing suspicious. Perhaps he was over-estimating Preiser, he thought. Perhaps Preiser wasn't really interested in him. He left the car and walked to the entrance to the Stadium. For a while, he stood in the entrance doorway. Again he saw nothing unforeseen. He purchased a spectator's ticket and went inside the Stadium. The rink was busy, the atmosphere lively, cool and noisy. For a few minutes he sat in the terraced rows of seats amongst other spectators and watched. But he wasn't watching the skaters, he was watching for Preiser's men. He didn't see any.

The coffee stall was behind the stand. It was run by a middle-aged woman who had a harassed and worried expression on her face. Stack waited until there was no one at the stall before making his move. He then went up to her.

'Frau Schoneberg?' he asked.

The woman eyed him up and down suspiciously. 'Who are you?' she asked.

'I'm a friend of Herr Criller,' Stack said quietly. The woman looked more harassed than before.

'Coffee?' she asked hurriedly, as if playing for time.

'Please.'

Stack knew that he had found the right person. She hadn't denied her knowledge of Criller. She was trying to sort out in her mind what Stack's motives could be. A party of skaters gathered around. Stack stood to one side and allowed them to be served first. When they were alone again the woman handed him his drink. He gave her the money.

'What do you want with Herr Criller?' the woman whispered.

'To help him,' Stack replied.

Again the woman eyed him suspiciously. Stack drank his coffee. It had a sweet taste. He wished she had left it without sugar.

'I finish in half an hour,' she said quietly.

'I will wait,' Stack said.

The woman started to busy herself with the coffee machine. Stack caught a frightened look on her face as he walked away. He stood to one side, drinking his coffee. Something, or somebody, had got Frau Schoneberg frightened. He sensed danger. Perhaps Preiser was being cleverer than he thought. Perhaps Preiser was giving him rope to play with. Perhaps... He stopped contemplating Preiser's movements and switched to cursing his own stupidity. The coffee had been fixed. He could feel himself becoming drowsy. Frau Schoneberg had fixed it. He had to get out of the building. His vision became blurred. He staggered towards the exit. Faces loomed up in front of him. Hands grabbed at him. He pushed them aside. He had to get out of the building. Something gripped him. He tried to shake it off. There was a sharp pain in his arm. He staggered forward. He had to get out. He had to...

Stack fell to the ground, and Preiser and his two assistants stood over him. Preiser had a smug, satisfied expression on his face...

Stack's first recollections, after his unconscious state, was of half-awakening, as if from a deep sleep, feeling sickly and looking into a yellow sea. He was lying on his back, he thought, and the yellow sea was electric lights. He closed his eyes again. He heard a man's voice, but the words didn't make sense. They were just a jumble of words. He tried to ignore them, but the jumble became coherent. They began to register in his brain, '...we have come a long way from the use of simple barbiturate and amphetamine drugs,' the voice said proudly. 'Doctor Würnberg, who heads the Neuropsychopharmocology Department at our University Research Institute, has become a leading exponent of new psychotropic drugs. He has gone far beyond the bounds of any leading Western specialist with his experiments. Of course, he has been encouraged to do so, and he has had a lot of support and help from the department in the Moscow Medical Research Centre. They too are very interested in this field, Herr Stack, as you will appreciate.'

Stack opened his eyes to see Preiser's sickly, smiling face in front of him. He closed his eyes again.

'Your brain is like any other piece of

machinery,' Preiser went on. 'It has component parts. At the moment some of your component parts are not functioning. However, Doctor Würnberg has been able to isolate and control certain functions of the brain by the use of selective drugs.' Stack tried to close his mind to Preiser's words, but he couldn't. 'The names of these drugs would just confuse you,' Preiser said smugly, 'but you are about to go on a journey, Herr Stack, that would be the envy of many of the drug addicts of your decadent society. Whilst one part of your brain will be in a state of sleep, another part will be roused through a state of excitement to panic. You will tell us all we want to know, Herr Stack, and you will relive a lifetime in a matter of minutes. You are about to undergo a unique experience.'

There was a pregnant silence. Stack desperately urged himself to fight against any capitulation. He told himself that he didn't know anything, and that he worked for Roberts of Military Intelligence. He felt something cool touch his arm, followed by a sharp jab. The drug was being injected into his system, he thought. He looked up into the yellow lights and his vision became blurred. He began to float into another world. Float and drift. He felt relaxed and happy – really happy – overjoyed. The feeling swelled inside of him. He laughed and shouted at the children's faces that appeared before him. He saw the seashore and a group of teenagers. The figures grabbed him, and together they rolled over in a kaleidoscopic jumble of people, sea, sand, green fields, and red brick houses. The whirlpool of fantasy stopped at rows of red-tiled roofs, like the figures on a fruit machine. Rows and rows of red-tiled roofs – the symbol of the suburbia of his youth. And there were faces, all sorts of faces. They kept vanishing and appearing in front of him. Some faces were familiar, others were unknown to him. He had both the power of visual recognition and of sensual feeling. There were moments of great elation and moments of deep sadness. He felt himself crying bitterly over a face that was unrecognisable, and at another time laughing, uncontrollably, with faces that also meant nothing to him. The sensual feelings, and kaleidoscopic visions, were interspersed by moments of apparent sanity. He was in a room. There was a bed and a side table. On the table was a green water jug and a glass. And there were three other men in the room. One was Preiser – Stack's very dear friend, Heltman Preiser. They all laughed together. Good old Preiser. Preiser, Stack's friend. Preiser who had done so much for Stack. Preiser, dear Preiser. The two other men were Preiser's friends. Everybody was a friend. Stack sat on the side of the bed, the others stood around him. They listened intently to his stories. They laughed with him. They looked sad when he felt sad. They were his friends. But there was no consciousness of sound – no sound. It was happening, but he couldn't hear it. Then the whirlpool would suddenly transcend him into the realms of fantasy again. Into visions of his past. Into moments of his immediate past – to visions of Sue, and to visions which he had forgotten...

The visions and dreams became a nightmare. It became unbearable. It was like being on a never-ending treadmill. He began to feel panic. Would it never end? Would it never end? He wanted to get off. Get off... Get off... Get off...

Suddenly he was awake. He was awake and he knew that he was normal. His eyes were closed, but all else was normal. He had been given drugs to make him give up his secrets. His brain told him that. It flashed messages to him, crisply, like a well-charged battery. It was all crystal clear. You are lying on a bed with your eyes closed, he told himself. You have recovered from the effect of the drugs. You are not fastened to the bed; there are no restrictions. But you are still Preiser's captive, so you must think of escape. Think of escape! What did I tell them, he asked himself? Tell me first, what did I tell them? About Berak? Yes, he thought. He had told them about Berak, and of their meetings in

Prague and Berlin, and of Berak's link with Colonel Zeiler of the Czech Secret Service. Yes, he had told them all that, he thought. And what else? He had told them that Berak had two informers – Colonel Zeiler, and Wilhelm Boucher of the East German Foreign Service. He had also told them of Berak's final messages passed at the Press gatherings. Messages which warned of a Russian interest in the Balkans. An interest brought about by their need to have bases in the Mediterranean for their Fleet. A Fleet to match the U.S. Sixth Fleet, with established bases, that would swing the balance of power in their favour.

Stack lay quite still as his brain unfolded its confessions. He had told them how Berak had passed his messages, he thought, and how Stack had posted his messages to Control. And about Roberts, he thought, but they would know about him. What else, he asked himself? What else had he told them? His brain responded. He had told them that something had gone wrong in Berlin, that there was a leak. Colonel Zeiler had been arrested. So had others. Berak had become anxious for his own safety. He had wanted to defect. Stack had urged him to remain. Boucher had got wind of something big. Something very big. So big that it was even going to be kept from the Warsaw Pact Ministers' meeting in East Berlin. Something that Stack had to know about. Berak had persuaded Gunter to take over, and Stack had tried to help Berak to escape. He had gone to Lieffer about it, but neither Stack nor Lieffer had been able to help. Berak had made his own plans and Berak was dead. Yes, Stack thought, he had told them all that. Berak had been shot, dead, and Stack had forced himself to forget about Berak and concentrate on Gunter. Gunter! What about Gunter, Stack wondered? What had he told them about Gunter? What did he remember? There was the excited look on Gunter's face, he thought. It had only been ten days after Gunter had taken over. Gunter had been excited and scared. Boucher had been on to him. There was still a leak! Boucher was under suspicion. Gunter was uncertain. Stack had forced his hand. Gunter had to go back to Boucher, and get what he could from him.

Stack breathed heavily, his eyes still closed. He could see Gunter's face quite clearly. How did Gunter make his pass, he wondered? He got no answer. How did Gunter make his pass, he asked himself again? Again he got no answer. It was still a blank. He mentally sighed. What else do you remember, he asked himself hurriedly? There was Gunter's anxious face, he thought. He remembered that. Gunter had to get to Boucher before meeting Stack in Spain. Spain! Yes,

Stack remembered. They were to meet in Spain. Think of Spain, he told himself. He could see the mountains and the aeroplane wreckage. That would be Gunter's plane, he thought. What had Stack been looking for? And who was the figure in the dark suit? There had been a fight. Yes, he remembered, a fight with a man, and he remembered Doctor Lorenzo. Go back to the wreckage, he said to himself. What had happened there? What had happened?... But it wouldn't come. It wouldn't come. He had told them all that he had known. About Berak, about Gunter, and about his contact with Control. They knew as much as he did now, he thought. They knew that he didn't know what great secret Gunter had been going to unfold for him! He had failed. He had wasted all that time and energy. He had even sacrificed their contact in the East German Foreign Office. He had failed. The side effects would be marginal in the spy game, he thought. The losses would be quite small, other than the prize of finding out what Boucher had got on to. That loss would hurt, he thought, when the effects of the drugs wore off. That was what his work in Berlin had been about. That was why Berak was dead. The numbness and guilt would return. He wasn't going to be free of them, yet. He mentally groaned. There was still Schmidt and the organisation, he thought. He might still be able to salvage some self respect out of his failure, if he could get to them. He had to think of escape. He had to get out of Preiser's clutches. He lay quite still, and tried to pick up any sound that would indicate whether or not he was being observed. He knew he was lying on a mattress, but there was no hospital smell about the room. The atmosphere had a foisty smell.

He heard no sound at all. Very slowly, he opened his eyes, moving the lids, fractionally, to disclose a blurred, yellow light. He wasn't in a hospital, he thought. They had taken him elsewhere. He opened his eyes fully, and they focused on a bare, electric light bulb hanging on a short length of flex above his head. He moved his head to one side and saw bare floor boards, dirty walls and a panelled door. He became fully alert. He had been taken to a room where he was being kept a prisoner, he thought. He struggled to an upright position. The room was about four metres square. He was on an iron-framed, hospital-type bed. He looked about him. The ceiling had once been ornate and decorated. It was now dirty and falling apart. So was the wall plaster. A window opening was covered with dark brown woodwork that matched the door. Where was he, he wondered? Where had they taken him? He let his feet fall over the edge of the bed. They were like lead weights attached to the lower part of his body. He remained seated on the bed. His body felt weak and tired, but his brain was alert and active. They had got all they wanted out of him, he thought. They knew all that he knew. Now they were finished with him. But surely they wouldn't keep him prisoner. They would have to release him when the questions were asked – or would they?

He stood upright. His head swam and his legs sagged. He sat down again. A noise outside the door sharply attracted his attention. It was as if his senses were magnified. The door handle turned. He watched it, his pulse quickening. The door opened. He held his breath. A figure appeared. It was Preiser! He came into the room. The two men looked at each other.

'How do you feel?' Preiser asked. There was no visible sign of satisfaction on his face. It was expressionless.

'Lousy,' Stack replied grimly.

'It will pass very soon,' Preiser said. 'You will soon feel well enough to leave.'

'Leave? Where are you taking me?'

Preiser shrugged. 'Nowhere,' he said.

Stack didn't understand the situation.

'You will be free to leave,' Preiser explained.

'Where am I?' Stack asked suspiciously.

'East Berlin,' Preiser said.

Stack's hand went to his pockets. He knew

there was a catch. He wasn't mistaken. His passport was missing!

'My passport,' he said.

Preiser looked concerned.

'Oh,' he said. 'It must have dropped out of your pocket when you took ill.'

'When I took ill?' Stack growled.

'In the Ice Stadium,' Preiser explained calmly.

Stack glowered at him. If he had felt better, he would have taken his resentment out on the man, physically.

'If you report the loss,' Preiser went on, 'we will do all we can to help you recover it.'

Again Stack glowered.

'How am I supposed to return to West Berlin?' he asked.

Preiser looked thoughtful.

'I should give the authorities in West Berlin a telephone call from an hotel,' he said. 'Or phone your office.' He smiled. 'It is really a minor problem.'

'Minor compared with what the Party is planning?' Stack asked.

'Precisely,' Preiser replied.

'Just what are you planning?' Stack asked.

Preiser smiled, as if to say that he wasn't going to be drawn. He put his hand in his pocket and withdrew a silver cigarette case. Stack's eyes watched him closely. The cigarette case! It was not unlike his own, he thought. He watched Preiser flick it open.

Something inside Stack's brain clicked into place. The wheels started to move.

'Cigarette, Herr Stack?' Preiser asked.

Cigarette! Gunter! Stack's brain began to shriek at him. Today is Monday, so take the second cigarette from the left! Automatically his hand went out. He watched his fingers pick out the second cigarette from the hinged end of the case. Preiser stood smiling. My God! Stack thought. The cigarette case under his pillow in the hotel bedroom. That was it! That was what he had collected from the air crash. Gunter's cigarettes! His brain seemed to accelerate into action. It flashed him a picture of the scene of the air crash. Bodies and wreckage were strewn over the mountainside. He could see himself with a group of uniformed Spanish police searching the bodies. They had found Gunter – his head had been sliced from his body, but Stack had found his cigarette case. The police had wanted the case – Stack had handed it over, but had kept the cigarettes and put them in his own case! And he still had them, he thought. He still had them! He had never smoked them! He put Preiser's cigarette to his lips. He smoked little, but it had been Gunter's way of passing on the information. He could see it all clearly. Gunter would place the micro film of his coded message inside a cigarette. At the press meetings, he would offer Stack a cigarette, and Stack would know which one to take. Stack felt like laughing out aloud. Preiser's psychotropic drugs had stimulated Stack's brain, and Preiser's action had unconsciously triggered off the mechanism of Stack's lost memory. They had unwittingly told him what he had wanted to know. They had given him back his past! Again he had to stop himself from giving anything away. He let the smoke trickle into his mouth and he blew it out. If Gunter had made his preparation for the switch in Spain, he thought, the information would have been written on one of the cigarettes still in Stack's cigarette case! He felt the excitement mounting. The cigarette case in his hotel bedroom in West Berlin!

'Are you all right?' Preiser asked.

Stack looked up at him.

'The cigarette has gone to my head,' he said, and hurriedly warned himself against saying anything foolhardy. Now that he knew where to find the information, he had to make sure nothing went wrong.

'How much did I tell you?' he asked. He found the cigarette distasteful and put it out.

This time Preiser was more communicative.

'Unfortunately – or fortunately – you do not know very much,' he said.

'So why don't you just let me return to West Berlin?' Stack asked.

'But we will,' Preiser replied airily. He threw his cigarette to the floor and stamped it out. 'As soon as you feel fit enough to travel, you may leave.' He backed away from the door. *'Auf wiedersehen,* Herr Stack,' he said formally, and left Stack alone in the room.

Stack looked at the door and frowned. They weren't just going to let him go, he thought. There was a catch somewhere. He struggled to his feet. He felt fractionally better, but not fit enough to walk out of the room. He sat down again and waited. Preiser had said Stack's tiredness would pass. He slapped his knees impatiently. He had to get back to West Berlin, he thought. He had to! He could feel himself becoming agitated, and forced himself to sit calmly on the bed. After a short while he was able to make his move. He walked to the door and hesitated. A hail of lead could greet him. He swallowed hard and decided to take precautions. He flattened himself against the wall, and with an outstretched hand turned the door handle. It responded to his action and he pulled the door open. The door creaked on its hinges and swung open, but there was no hail of lead. Only a feeling of inky blackness. He breathed heavily and moved into the opening, but Preiser wasn't going to let him walk out, he thought. It wasn't going to be as easy as that. He moved cautiously on to the landing. It was in darkness. From the light of the room that he had left, he could see that the building was an empty terraced dwelling house. He stood on top of the staircase, the perspiration rolling down his back. Any second he expected a bullet from a revolver to blast him into eternity. He stepped gingerly on to the first tread; it creaked under his weight. The handrail and balustrade moved as he put his weight on them. He slowly descended the staircase, his eyes frantically searching the darkness for any sign of movement, and his ears strained for any tell-tale noise. A tread collapsed under his weight, and he went crashing forward. The delicately fixed balustrade stopped his fall. He lay on a half landing cursing himself, and anxiously listening for any reactions. There were none. He continued his way down the staircase, his mind warning him that there was a catch somewhere. It couldn't happen, he thought. He just couldn't walk out of an interrogation with Preiser. It just couldn't be.

He came to the ground floor. There was a narrow passageway. He stealthily inspected it. At one end was the main entrance door, at the other – an empty room which opened on to a yard. It was dark outside, except when the moon flitted between the clouds. He stood quite still in the passageway. Preiser wanted him to leave the building, he thought. Even perhaps the district. But Stack knew that he was a dead duck. Somewhere they would get him. His time was limited. But he didn't give up. No one gives up at that stage. He weighed up the situation. He could stay where he was and sweat it out. Preiser would close in. Stack would then be trapped inside the building. They would already have the roof under observation. He wouldn't get out that way. The alternative was to go out into the open. That was what they wanted. At some place of their choosing they would eliminate him. It might be a car accident, a rifle-bullet in the back, or even an accident on the subway. So what did he do, he asked himself? He favoured going out into the open. No one would want to die in that foul-smelling building, he thought. At least he would die in the open. Which way? Rear or front? The rear was the obvious way, he thought, and decided to take the front.

The front door was unlocked. He pulled it open and felt naked on the threshold. No hail of lead. He breathed easier, relaxed his shoulders, and hurried down a short flight of steps and on to the pavement. He didn't hesitate on the pavement. He turned left, for no reason at all, and walked quickly away from the building. He came to a crossroad and took stock of his surroundings. The buildings were tall. Most were occupied. The area was badly illuminated. In the distance he could hear traffic. To his right was an open piece of waste land. Then he saw one of them and his heart sank. It was just a movement in the shadows along the street to his left. He went in the opposite direction. He walked slowly, listening for a sign of danger. A motor car entered the square, and he saw two more of them in its headlamps. They were closing in on him. He increased his pace. Where was he going? He was lost. A door opened; a woman yelled abuse and the door closed again. A dog barked and a motor-cycle engine coughed into life. All typical city noises. Stack heard them, but imagined others. The sound of feet getting closer. The metallic click of automatics being loaded. He came to a cross road and saw street lights in the distance. If he could only reach them, he would be safe, he thought. They looked warm and bright, but two figures were silhouetted against the bright background. There was no escape. He couldn't turn back, they were behind him. He moved forward, keeping in the shadows. A hand suddenly grabbed at him. His heart missed a beat. He quickly jerked himself away from the hand, and the figure in the shadow.

'It is Schmidt!' a voice hissed desperately.

Schmidt! Stack stopped dead in his tracks. Could it really be Schmidt? He felt the hand grab him again. It pulled him into the shadows.

'Schmidt?' Stack asked unbelievingly.

'Yes,' Schmidt hissed. Stack's relief was enormous. 'Hurry!' Schmidt said urgently, and pulled Stack along a narrow lane. Stack didn't need any second bidding. They came to a brick air shaft. Schmidt pulled Stack behind it, as two bullets smacked into the brickwork. There were more shots fired. The lane re-echoed to the crack and whine of flying bullets. But they were firing wild.

'My car is at the end of the lane,' Schmidt hissed. 'Now run!'

He gave Stack a push. Stack shot forward, darting from side to side. He could feel Schmidt hot on his heels. More shots were fired, and several bullets whined past, perilously close to their heads. They reached the dark shape of the car and got inside. Schmidt started the engine and the car lurched forward. He switched on the head-lamps and picked out two figures who jumped to one side as the car shot through them. The rear window was suddenly shattered by a bullet. Stack dropped his head. So did Schmidt. Schmidt drove furiously, swinging the car around the open, demolished site, like an expert. Stack hung on to the handle on the dashboard. They swung into another street and came to a street with lights. The tension inside the car eased.

'That was close,' Schmidt sighed. 'We are free of them!'

Were they really free of them, Stack wondered? He looked behind him, through the gap in the rear widow. There was no one on their tail. Thank God for that, he sighed.

'But we can't be certain,' Schmidt warned. He turned off the main thoroughfare and followed a route through the deserted, half-demolished side streets.

'Where are you taking me?' Stack asked.

'That depends on you,' Schmidt replied. 'Where do you want to go?'

'West Berlin,' Stack said. 'And fast.'

'We can only take you through Criller's channel,' Schmidt replied. 'It would take too long to arrange any other way.'

Stack silently swore. He had to get to West Berlin as quickly as possible. He had to get Gunter's message before it was too late, but he had to play it carefully. To arouse Schmidt's curiosity could prove dangerous.

'Criller?' Stack asked suspiciously. 'You mean I take his place?'

'You go with him. He is at the hotel.'

'With him? Has Criller been contacted?'

Schmidt turned his scraggy face in Stack's direction.

'You sound surprised,' he said.

'I am,' Stack replied. He hadn't been able to get near to Criller. Preiser had seen to that. Yet Criller had still got to the rendezvous.

'Criller has paid his fee,' Schmidt said. 'He is at the meeting place. We can look after him now.'

'I didn't tell him where to go,' Stack pointed out.

'Then someone else did,' Schmidt said firmly. Again he looked at Stack. 'Do not concern yourself,' he said pointedly.

In other words, forget it, Stack thought. Somebody else had made the contact. Someone else had got to Criller. Who, Stack wondered? Who else could it have been?

'I thank you for saving me from Preiser's men,' he said. 'To say the least, I am grateful.'

'Save your gratitude,' Schmidt said with smile. 'I will be well paid when you get back to West Berlin.'

'Well paid? Stack asked suspiciously. 'By whom?'

Schmidt shook his head and looked serious.

'No further questions,' he said sternly. 'No more talk.'

8

Stack and Criller sat in the bedroom watching each other. Stack saw Criller rubbing his wrist. Criller then removed his spectacles from his face and rubbed the bridge of his nose as if the spectacles were causing an irritation. Stack was suspicious. Suspicious of Lehna, of Preiser, of Schmidt. Suspicious of everything, and it all stemmed from the man calling himself Criller. With Criller everything was wrong. He didn't look German. He didn't look Jewish, and he certainly didn't look like a man about to embark upon a new career and marriage. The only thing that tied up with what Lehna had told Stack about him were the spectacles. Nothing else seemed to fit. Criller was much smaller than Stack, and more heavily built. He had jet black hair, a dark, swarthy skin, and dark eyes. His face was square, his eyes wide apart, and his command of the German language restricted to certain essentials. Lehna's description of her fiancé had pictured a tall, youthful, intelligent engineer. What had confronted Stack when he had entered the room was a surly, tense, middle-aged man, and the muzzle of an automatic revolver.

Stack had overcome his initial surprise and established his identity, and link, with the man. They had taken up a stance of mutual distrust, and watched each other as they waited for their contact to take charge of them.

Stack thought back to Lehna. She was dark and attractive. He had accepted her as being an Israeli, but on reflection she could also have come from a Balkan country. She could have been equally Hungarian, Rumanian, or a Yugoslav, and so could Criller. Stack had accepted her identity, and her intentions, on their face value. Now he wondered about them. He also wondered what her motives had been in trying to prevent him from contacting Criller. Had she realised that Stack's suspicions would have been immediately aroused? Had she realised that he would have questioned her more closely? Was that why she had tried to make him believe that she had left Berlin?

Stack sat quietly smouldering. He'd walked straight into Preiser's trap in the Ice Stadium. That puzzled him. So did Schmidt's timely intervention. Had Schmidt actually saved his life? Had someone really hired Schmidt? Had Stack got himself into the dingy hotel bedroom with Criller by a series of accidents? Or had he got himself there by someone else's design?

The problems never left Stack as he waited for the next move.

Shortly after two a.m., their contact came for them. He was a heavily built man with short, shaven hair, and dressed in a green boiler suit. He didn't waste any time on introductions. Brusquely he ordered them to follow him.

They left the hotel via a rear door and crossed an open yard. Waiting for them was a large, container-type truck. Another man sat in the driver's seat and kept the engine running. Their contact opened a side door and Stack and Criller got into the container. It was filled with crates and boxes. A small electric bulb gave off a dull light. Criller crouched in one corner and Stack sat in another. There was no dialogue, or bond, between them. Only suspicion.

The truck started on its journey. Stack felt trapped on a course of action that was not to his liking, but he knew that there was little he could do about it. He made himself as comfortable as possible on the hard, ribbed floor, and slept fitfully as the night passed. There were a number of stops during the early morning, but it was not until mid-day that they finally reached their destination. The access door was flung open and they were ordered to get out. Gladly they left the container and stretched their legs in the open air. They were in a courtyard of a large farm. Their contact was standing beside an open door to a farm building. The driver joined them. He was smaller than his companion and softer spoken.

'In the basement,' he ordered. 'You will be picked up at 21.00 hours.'

Criller moved to the doorway. As he stepped into the building their contact gave him a bundle of clothing.

'Put these on,' he growled. He turned to Stack. 'And you,' he said.

Stack accepted the clothes. They were a pair of dark, rough trousers and a dark jacket.

'Leave your own clothes in the room,' the man ordered.

Stack followed Criller down a flight of wooden steps into the basement. No sooner had they entered the room than the door was closed and bolted behind them.

Stack glanced about him. The room was lit by an electric light bulb, which hung over a wooden table. On the table was some food and wine. There was also a couple of beds with bare mattresses, and several newspapers. The walls were whitewashed, but bare. The floor was stone slabs, and there was a dry smell of corn.

'We could be worse,' he said.

Criller looked at him. Stack waved an arm about the room and repeated his statement. Criller looked away, and started to change his clothing. Stack went over to a bed and did likewise. He could see the wisdom of wearing rough, dark clothes. Especially Criller, whose coloured shirt would have been conspicuous. Stack changed his clothes. They fitted reasonably well, but the jacket sleeves were short. He glanced at Criller. He was also having similar trouble, except that his jacket sleeves were too long.

Stack went up to him and held out his jacket.

'Try this one,' he said. 'It looks more your size.'

Criller looked at him sharply.

'No,' he said, shaking his head. 'No.'

'Come on,' Stack insisted. 'Yours will probably fit me better.'

He tried to push the jacket on to Criller. Criller swung around and knocked the jacket out of Stack's hand. The two men eyed each other. Stack saw the anger in Criller's eyes. He looked as if he was sparring for a fight.

'What's troubling you?' Stack asked, relieving the tension.

'I said, no,' Criller replied in broken German.

'I was just being friendly,' Stack said, eyeing him closely.

Criller scowled and turned away. Stack picked up his own jacket and returned to his bed. Criller's attitude puzzled him. Everything about Criller puzzled him. The only thing that was certain about Criller was that he was not what Lehna had described. Either Lehna had been lying, or this wasn't the real Criller.

Thoughtfully Stack lay on the bed, his hands holding the jacket. His fingers touched a piece of material that was different from the rest of the jacket. He glanced at it. It was a small strip of leather across the shoulders, but it had a rough touch, like fine sandpaper. He glanced across at Criller. He was sitting at the table eating some of the food. There was no patch on the back of his jacket. Stack's suspicions were aroused. What was the need for the patch, he wondered? It wasn't large enough to protect the shoulders from any chafing, and it had a strange feel about it. He put on the jacket and lay as if resting. Criller wouldn't accept the jacket, he thought, although it was more suitable for him. Why was that? Was there some special reason why he preferred the other jacket? Was there some particular reason? Was Stack's jacket a marked jacket? Stack's pulse quickened. Berak had been shot in his attempted escape. The West German border guard had referred to an orange flash like a trip flare. Orange flash! Could Berak's jacket have been marked with a fluorescent material that could be picked out by the beam of a searchlight? Stack's pulse did a double beat. That was it, he thought! That was it! Berak's jacket had been marked, and so was Stack's. Marked so that it would be picked out by the beam of a searchlight! Marked so that the person wearing it could be shot in their attempted escape. Stack's inside turned over. He felt as if he had been kicked in the stomach. He was a man about to be executed! A man whose life expectancy was only a few hours. He felt weak as it all began to fit into place. Preiser had let him go free, knowing that Schmidt would pick him up. Why should Preiser risk an international scandal when Schmidt and his organisation would do the deed for him? Schmidt would get Stack to the border, and the border guards would have a legitimate excuse to shoot him. Stack would be an escaping refugee from the East. How were the guards to know who he was? Here was Stack in the dress of a country workman, attempting to cross the border illegally. Preiser's hands were clean.

Stack breathed heavily. That meant that Schmidt, or someone else, was in league with Preiser. He grunted audibly. That was where he had come in. That was why Berak had been murdered. Someone was giving the Communists the tip off. Someone knew about Stack. That someone had now tipped off Preiser. When they had finished with Stack, Preiser had gone through his pantomime. Stack had fallen into the trap like a fool. Instead of going to an hotel and contacting the Western authorities, he had let Schmidt take over. And now Stack was past the point of no return. Criller began to take on another guise now. Criller was in the plot. He was on Preiser's side. He knew that Stack was a marked man. That was why he had refused the jacket. Stack swallowed hard. He was going to have to discard the jacket before they entered the open ground, he thought. He glanced at his nylon shirt. That wasn't going to give much protection. It would soon be picked out. So he would have to think of something else. He watched Criller at the table. Criller's hand kept touching his bulging jacket pocket, as if checking that his revolver was still there. Somehow they were going to have to make a switch, Stack thought. Somehow they were going to change jackets...

At nine o'clock, precisely, their door was unbarred. Stack hadn't decided how, or when, he and Criller were going to exchange jackets, but he was more determined than ever that there was going to be a switch. The younger of their two contacts greeted them in quiet tones. He had changed from his green boiler suit into dark clothes, similar to those that Criller and Stack were wearing. They left the basement. In the courtyard stood a small, dark saloon. Inside was their other guide. Stack was hustled into the rear seat alongside Criller. Their contact got into the driver's seat and drove out of the court-yard.

Stack watched the countryside. It was fertile, undulating ground of fields and woods. Their route followed a series of narrow secondary roads, sometimes only farm tracks, which skirted the thick pine woods. Perhaps he should make a break for it there and then, he thought desperately. There was plenty of cover, and they wouldn't be expecting the move. The car door was not locked. But would he be allowed to get away with it? Would they let him remain at large? He shuffled about in his seat. He had to decide now whether to make a break for it or take his chances on switching with Criller. It was now or never. The decision was suddenly made for him.

'We are here,' the driver said gruffly, and stopped the car.

They were alongside a wood. So it was going to be the switch, Stack thought grimly. It was going to be either him or Criller.

They got out of the car. Stack could feel the tension beginning to build up inside him. Somehow, somewhere, he had to make his move. Another figure suddenly loomed up out of the darkness. It was an East German border guard! Stack froze, but the others were unmoved. The two guides and the guards held a brief conversation. Stack and Criller stood to one side. The guard grunted and disappeared into the woods. The two guides came up to Stack and Criller. The younger of the two spoke in his quiet, country accent.

'I will take you to the border now,' he said. 'The time is precisely,' he glanced at his watch, 'twenty-one forty-eight.' Criller and Stack adjusted their watches. 'The timing is important,' the guide explained. 'When you pass through the first barrier fence, you will make for a thin strip of wood. It is about fifty metres from the fence. At the far side of the wood is a stream. Beyond the stream you will see the silhouette of a church.'

Church! Stack's inside reacted. Berak had been shot near a deserted churchyard at Fenstadt.

'You must make for the church. One you reach the churchyard you are in West Germany.'

'What is the name of the village at the other side?' Stack asked.

The guide looked at him. 'Fenstadt,' he said.

Fenstadt! Stack felt the blood drain away from his body.

'There are control towers to your right and left, about four hundred metres apart,' the guide explained. 'You must go direct to the church. If you deviate, you could set off a trip flare that will bring out the search-lights from both control towers.'

Criller grunted his agreement. Stack was surprised that he understood so readily.

'The timings are very important,' their contact added quietly. He sounded like a bored guide who had done it so many times before. Stack began to hate him.

'You pass the barriers at 22.00 hours. You reach the copse five minutes later. From there it is safer that you move one at a time.'

One at a time! Stack wondered why. It made him more suspicious. Safer for whom, he wondered? For Criller?

'At 22.10 precisely you leave the copse,' the guide said to Stack. 'It will take you five minutes to get to the church.' The man turned to Criller. 'You will follow at 22.20 precisely.'

After he had reached the church, Stack thought grimly. After he had been shot, dead! He felt like a trapped animal.

'At the church you will both be picked up by the West German border guards,' their guide added. 'You have the times?'

They both said that they had.

'Repeat them,' the man said to Stack.

Stack repeated his instructions. The guide turned to Criller. 'You fully understand?'

Criller gave a guttural, 'Yes,' in German. Again Stack wondered how he could understand so readily. Unless he had gone through the instructions elsewhere, Stack thought.

'Good,' their guide said gruffly. 'The

control tower to the north,' he pointed to his right with his arm outstretched, 'will probably be scanning their area at twenty-three hundred hours. You will both be out of their range. The tower to the south will also be scanning their area some time before midnight. Again you will be safe.'

Stack listened intently.

'There will be a patrol returning along this area at twenty-two thirty precisely,' the guide added, and looked pointedly at both Criller and Stack. 'They have dogs,' he warned. 'The dogs will get your scent and they will be let loose. You must,' he emphasised his words. 'You must be clear of the stream by twenty-two thirty. It is essential. Between the fence and the woods is still East German territory.'

Stack knew now when he had to make his move. It was before the dogs could be let loose on him, and before he went out into the open.

'Come,' the guide said gruffly, and moved into the woods. Criller followed behind. Stack hesitated, momentarily, saw the other guide watching him closely, and moved into the woods behind Criller.

It was pitch black amongst the trees. The guide stopped to allow them to get used to the darkness, and then moved forward, slowly and stealthily. Criller and Stack kept close together. Stack's heart began to thump wildly, his brain warning him that if he didn't take action, he was going to his own execution, just as Berak had gone to his. Berak hadn't known, but Stack did. He had to do something about it.

Suddenly they were through the wood, and the darkness gave way to the dull, grey light of the open countryside. Occasionally the moon appeared between the clouds. In front of them loomed a high wire fence. In the distance a dog barked as if giving them a timely warning. Stack breathed heavily. Criller stood beside him.

The guide touched Stack's shoulder and waved him to the ground. Stack and Criller went to earth. The guide got down beside them and pulled a large tuft of earth towards him. Silently he indicated that they were to crawl under the wire and follow a line directly ahead of them. Another pat on Stack's shoulder and he was ordered to make his move. Stack's mouth went dry. There was no turning back now, he thought. He flattened himself and crawled through the trench under the first barrier. He kept crawling to the second wire. There was a similar sinking in the ground, camouflaged by the grass, to give him access. Momentarily he stopped – almost expecting to see an armed guard on top of him. Criller came up behind him and urged him forward with his hand on Stacks's foot. Stack cleared the fence. Ahead of them was the open ground. Somewhere to his right and left were control towers, with searchlights. He moved forward, inching his way over the ground, using every bit of cover and caressing the ground with every muscle of his body. Slowly the copse loomed up in front of him. Again a dog barked, and then silence enveloped the area. It was an eerie silence. The silence that warns the animal kingdom of danger. It warned Stack as well. He crawled cautiously into the copse, his hands feeling gingerly for any trip-wires that would set off a flare or anti-personnel mine. He touched something hard and cold. His inside froze. Was it a small mine? His fingers nervously examined the object. It was only a stone, the size of his fist. He gave a long sigh of relief and his pulse resumed its normal beat. But the stone could be useful, he thought. He kept it in his hand as he moved forward through the bushes that formed a barrier between the tall trees.

Criller came in beside him. They stood up, alongside each other, both breathing heavily with the physical exercise and tenseness. Stack noticed that Criller had discarded his spectacles. Criller moved forward, taking the lead. Stack watched, momentarily, and then followed. The copse was thick with overgrown bushes that caught their clothing and restricted their movement. They were almost prisoners to the clinging vines. It became a nightmare. Eventually they came to the clearing at the far side.

'There is the church,' Criller said in his brusque, broken German, and pointed to his front. Stack peered into the distant greyness, but it took a short while before his eyes became adjusted. He saw the faint silhouette of the building.

'Now it is five minutes after ten,' Criller said gruffly, looking at his luminous watch. 'You move in five minutes.'

Stack nodded his head, but he was wondering how Criller had suddenly acquired such good eyesight. That settled it, he thought. That was the excuse he had wanted for himself. He edged himself, quickly, into a position behind Criller, and mustered all his energy. As Criller half turned to see what he was doing, Stack brought his fist with the stone in it, down on the back of Criller's neck with all the force he could muster. His hand connected and sent shock waves up his arm, but Criller sank to the ground, unconscious.

The pain in Stack's arm was immediately forgotten. He bent over Criller and hurriedly removed Criller's jacket and dressed him in his own jacket. Criller stirred as Stack was putting the jacket on him. Stack stood up and put on his new jacket. In the pockets he found a torch and Criller's automatic. He put them in Criller's pockets. Criller stirred again. Stack bent down and gingerly moved the pointers of Criller's watch forward to read five minutes before the half-hour. If Criller accepted the time when he awoke, then he might take the lead and Stack could follow him.

Criller stirred again and groaned. He was coming to. The timing could not have been better, Stack thought. He quickly crept forward to the edge of the stream and slipped into the water. It seeped into his clothes, but it wasn't very deep. He crossed over to the far bank. It was sandy and provided a barrier against the open ground. He pressed his body into the dark, shadowy inlet and waited.

The minutes passed. There was no sound of any movement from Criller. Perhaps he was still dazed, Stack thought. He clenched his fists tensely and sweated. He would have been on the open ground now, approaching the church, he thought. A movement behind him in the bushes made him freeze. His perspiration became an ice-cold trickle down his back. Criller had recovered. More movement. Criller would be rubbing his neck, Stack thought. Now he would be feeling in his pocket for his revolver. Would he also be discarding his jacket? It all depended on how Criller reacted. He would be looking at his watch. Would he accept the time? Would he be prepared to move off? Would he be thinking about the dogs? There was a faint splash. Stack had got his answer. Criller was in the stream! Criller was on the move! Stack held his breath and sank into the bank, burying his face in the soft ground. He could hear Criller moving along the stream, but Criller was heading north! He was moving away from their directed route! He was taking his own route. The seconds ticked by. Stack remained frozen to the bank. He couldn't hear Criller any longer. Cautiously he moved himself away from the bank and looked at his watch. It was precisely 22.15 hours, the time that Stack should have been entering the church grounds.

No sooner had Stack checked the time, than the area surrounding the church suddenly sprang to life. The area was brilliantly illuminated from the beams of two powerful searchlights. Stack peered over the edge of the river bank. The open field was spread out before him like a floodlit football pitch, with the grey church building as the goalmouth. But the churchyard and buildings were not in West German territory, as Stack had been told. They were in the no-man's land between the two borders! Alongside the deserted church was the telltale tower with its searchlight. It would have been suicidal for Stack to have gone in that direction. The border fence did not run away to his left front, as he had been led to believe. It turned at an angle in the wood to appear again close to the church. Stack gritted his teeth. The bastards had tried to make him walk straight into their trap. But where was the West German border, he wondered? And peered into the blackness beyond the range of the searchlight. The searchlight from the church tower scanned the ground, as if looking for Stack. At the same instant, the dogs got the scent of the excitement and started barking aggressively. Their barking became wild and excited – and closer. The searchlight moved its beam back and forward over the field, as if in desperation. Suddenly another searchlight came to life. This time from a searchlight to the north of Stack's position. It was as if the whole area had been given orders to find Stack.

Brr! – Brr! – Brr! A burst of fire from a submachine gun made Stack lower his head. But they weren't firing at him. He peered over the top of the bank. There was another burst of automatic firing. Then Stack saw Criller! He was away to Stack's right – to the north – crawling over the ground. Stack felt his stomach turn over. There was a tell-tale orange glow on Criller's back that made him conspicuous. It was the death mark. Stack watched, like a spectator at a bull fight – disgusted, but helpless. Criller must have realised his danger. He started to remove his jacket.

'No!' Criller's voice cried out with feeling. 'No! It is...'

Brr! Brr! Brr!

Criller had shouted too late. As the jacket fell away from his hand, the bullets tore into his body. Criller lay on the ground, his body riddled with bullets.

Stack looked away. The guards had done what had been ordered of them. They had killed the man with the marking. Suddenly the lights went out. Pitch blackness enveloped the area. Only the dogs wouldn't be silenced. Their barking became almost frenzied. Stack had to make his move. He had to take his chance. He got out of the river bank and crawled on to the open ground. He turned in the direction that Criller had been following and ran across the open ground. In the distance he saw a single flash of light as if from a torch. It would be a signal for Criller, he thought, and gave it a wide berth.

9

It was very early in the morning when Stack landed at Tempelhof Airport, West Berlin, but despite the early hours, the military and police already had the area cordoned off and all vantage points manned. The atmosphere in the airport buildings was sharp, tense, reflecting the mood of the West Berlin authorities. Later that morning, the President of the People's Republic of Yugoslavia was arriving in West Berlin on a state visit, and some time during his stay in the city an assassination attempt was to be made on his life. That was the information Boucher had given Gunter. That was the message that Stack had been carrying about with him. That was the message his Control had electrified the German Federal Intelligence with, and brought Stack back to Berlin in a hurry. Such a threat was not totally unexpected by Western Intelligence Services. Yugoslavia was a country vulnerable to internal division. It was a country held together by the personality of their ageing President. Beneath the surface, the Serbs and the Croats eyed each other suspiciously. Only a spark was needed to ignite the flame that would start the uprising of the Southern Slavs to claim their independence. And it only needed such an uprising for the Russian machine to roll into the Balkans. The assassination of the Yugoslav President was planned to be the fuse to set off the uprising.

At the West German border, Stack had been fortunate. An astute young officer had granted his request to telephone Lieutenant Keller of the West Berlin *Kriminalpolitzei*. That one call had been sufficient to start the ball rolling, and it had rolled fast. Within minutes Stack was speaking to Roberts of the British Military Intelligence, and had passed on his instructions to Control about Gunter's message. Within two hours Stack was being flown back to the city in an aircraft of the West German Air Force.

Inside the airport building, Stack was hurried to an interview room. Two men were inside waiting for him. Roberts of British Military Intelligence and Hendrich Lieffer. They looked grim and concerned. It was the first time that Stack and Roberts had come face to face. Roberts was small, squat, and businesslike. Stack wasn't surprised at his presence. He knew that his Control needed someone to link up with the German Federal Intelligence, and Roberts was the ideal front man to operate through. Stack had also suspected that there was more to Lieffer than his role in the Ministry of Refugees, and in their line of business people didn't advertise their profession.

They got down to business immediately.

'From the beginning,' Roberts said crisply.

Stack went over his work from his contact with Berak and Gunter to his border crossing at Fenstadt. The two men listened intently to his every word. When he had finished, Roberts turned to Lieffer.

'The background to the assassination fits our intelligence reports,' he said. 'There have been Russian troop movements in Hungary, yesterday, under the guise of a military exercise. And we know the Russians are desperate to get another base for their Fleet.'

Lieffer nodded his head in agreement.

'Yes,' he said. 'It all fits into place. The question is – was this man Criller their assassin?'

'I feel certain that he was,' Stack said. 'That was why I was brought into their plans. I was their stooge. It wouldn't take much under-cover work to find out that I had arranged for Criller's escape and passage into West Germany.'

'No blame would be put on them,' Roberts added. 'It was a typical, Kremlin-engineered plot.'

'If what you say is true,' Lieffer said guardedly, 'we are now left with another problem. Will they have another assassin ready to do the deed?'

The three men exchanged furtive glances.

'Criller looked like a Serb,' Stack pointed out. 'He would have the necessary background to ignite an uprising. Can they find such a man again in a hurry?'

'Must it be such a man?' Lieffer posed. 'President Tito's assassination would still produce the required effects. It would be a little more clumsy, perhaps, but nevertheless...' He left the rest unsaid. The protection of the President must be Lieffer's responsibility, Stack thought. Lieffer was the Berlin Director of the Federal Counter Espionage as well as the Ministry of Refugees.

'There is one person who can tell us,' Roberts said.

'Fraulein Rosier?' Lieffer asked.

'Yes,' Roberts agreed.

Lehna, Stack thought! Yes, she would know. She would know a lot. If she would help them.

'Do you know where she is,' he asked.

Lieffer shook his head. 'No. She has disappeared, but she is still in Berlin.'

'Can you find her?' Roberts asked.

'A needle in a haystack,' Lieffer growled.

'Any information on the car registration number?' Stack asked. He was thinking of Schmidt. Schmidt was now a key man.

'A blank,' Roberts replied. 'It was a fictitious number.'

'And the other queries?' Stack asked.

Roberts looked at his watch. 'I should have them in a couple of hours,' he said. 'There have been delays.'

'Pass them to Herr Lieffer as soon as they are available,' Stack said. 'What about trying Lorenzo? He must know something.'

'We've already tried him out,' Lieffer said. 'After you gave me his name in my office, I got one of my men to visit him.'

'And?' Stack asked.

'Negative,' Lieffer growled. 'He doesn't know a Lehna Rosier, or a John Stack. Neither of you exist as far as Lorenzo is concerned.'

Stack gave a faint smile. Lorenzo was being true to his word. He wouldn't give anything away. He might to Stack, but there wasn't time to find out. Stack was beginning to like the large, fat man with the booming voice. He was a man of principles.

'Schmidt is the only one who can help us,' Roberts said.

'And I know where I can get hold of him,' Stack added. He turned to Lieffer. 'Can your men keep close to me in case of trouble?' he asked.

'We will keep close,' Lieffer said crisply, 'but the Communists will have heard of your escape.'

'Yes, they will,' Stack agreed, 'but they

don't know that we are aware of their assassination plot. When Preiser questioned me, I still had a blank. It was after his interrogation that it all came back to me.'

'Okay,' Roberts said briskly. 'Let's give it a try.' He withdrew a small automatic from his pocket and handed it to Stack. 'In case you run into trouble,' he said.

Stack pocketed the automatic. There was nothing more to be said. They could only play it as it came. They left the room. Stack made a quick call at his apartment to change his clothes, and then went to Schmidt's club in Spandau. In the bright sunlight of the early morning the bar took on an air less sinister and secretive than in the evening. Silently, a waiter swept the floor and cleared the ashtrays. Stack was the only occupant of the room. He sat over a coffee at the table where he had sat with Schmidt. He had made no request to the waiter to pass on any message, but his action was an invitation in itself. Half an hour later, Schmidt entered the room from a rear entrance behind the bar. He was smartly dressed, as if on his way to the office. He came over to Stack and they shook hands formally. Stack indicated a seat. Schmidt waved his hand and two coffees appeared.

'So you have returned safely,' Schmidt said, smiling.

'Criller was shot, dead, at the border,'

Stack pointed out.

Schmidt looked regretful.

'It should have been me,' Stack hissed. 'You double-crossed me.'

Schmidt looked hurt.

'No, Herr Stack,' he replied calmly. 'You were double-crossed, perhaps, but not by me.'

'Your organisation was responsible.'

Schmidt sat back.

'Come, Herr Stack,' he said. 'This is business. There are times when contracts do not always work out as planned.'

'Look, Herr Schmidt,' Stack said angrily, 'your organisation double deals. I don't like it.'

'So?' Schmidt asked. 'What do you suggest?'

'I know quite a lot about you and your organisation,' Stack said quietly. 'A lot the *Kriminalpolitzei* would like to get to know.'

Schmidt lit a cigar.

'That is a dangerous statement to make here in this room,' he said, between puffing at his cigar.

'Not really,' Stack said, tightlipped. 'I am not alone. I have two covers outside who could bring an army into the place if necessary.' He smiled faintly. 'I am not playing games any longer, Herr Schmidt. I haven't the time.'

'What do you want?' Schmidt asked.

'Two things,' Stack said. 'First, you and your organisation have a day off. Leave the field today. Let the big boys fight it out themselves.'

'And secondly?'

'Secondly, you tell me where I can find Fraulein Rosier.'

Schmidt's face remained impassive. He continued to smoke his cigar.

'What do I get in exchange?' he asked.

'I get off your back,' Stack said. 'When it is over, you might even be better off. You have a weak link somewhere, Herr Schmidt. It could prove dangerous for you.'

'And the alternative?'

'I sing like a canary.'

For a full two minutes neither man spoke. Finally Schmidt laid his cigar carefully in the ashtray.

'We have a good business here in Berlin,' he said sadly. 'It would be a pity to see it run into difficulties.'

He stood up.

'How is your wife these days?' he asked politely.

Sue! Stack looked at Schmidt. My God! Sue! Schmidt had warned him about her before. Was Sue involved? Was Schmidt telling the truth?

'She is well, I believe,' Stack replied calmly.

'That is good. She should be able to help you.'

Schmidt held out his hand.

'*Auf wiedersehen*, Herr Stack,' he said.

Stack accepted Schmidt's handshake.

'If you are lying to me, Herr Schmidt,' he hissed, 'I will be back looking for you.' Schmidt gave a faint smile. 'And I will find you,' Stack added menacingly.

'So be it,' Schmidt replied. He bowed his head, courteously, picked up his cigar, and left the bar by the rear exit.

Stack also left the bar. Outside the club entrance he hesitated, caught sight of his two covers, and hurriedly walked away from the area. There was a very strong possibility that Schmidt could not be trusted, he thought. Schmidt could have been playing for time.

At the corner of Carl Schutz Strasse, Stack picked up a taxi. He stayed with it for a couple of blocks, ditched it, and covered the rest of the journey by underground and taxi. If he lost his covers, he thought, then he would also lose any other tails that he might have. He arrived at Sue's apartment just before ten a.m. She never left for the studio before eleven.

Sue opened the entrance door to him. She was wearing her housecoat. Her face registered both surprise and delight.

'Oh! John,' she cried out. 'John! You are safe!'

She flung her arms around him.

Stack disengaged himself.

'Surprised?' he asked.

She stood back and looked at him. A hurt look came over her face as she saw his expression.

'What do you mean?' she asked.

Stack came into the apartment and closed the door.

'You know where I have been?' he asked.

'Yes,' she replied quietly.

He walked through the lounge into the bedroom.

'There is nobody here,' she called to him.

He ignored her remark and went from room to room. Sue stood watching him, a strained expression on her face. Stack looked out of the window and saw the cars parked in the square.

'Not working today?' he asked cynically.

'No,' she replied hotly.

'Ruddi not busy?'

'Yes, he is,' Sue replied, 'but he has gone to Bonn for Max on an assignment.'

'Bonn?' Stack asked, surprised. 'I thought Max was covering it?'

'Well, Ruddi is now. Max has remained in Berlin.'

So Ruddi had gone to Bonn for Max, Stack thought, and wondered why that should bother him.

'How did you know I was in the Eastern Sector?' he asked.

'Because a man came to the apartment and told me,' Sue snapped.

'What was he like?'

Sue gave her description of the man. It fitted Schmidt.

'When was this?'

'Yesterday afternoon.'

After Schmidt had engineered his escape, Stack thought.

He looked at her suspiciously. He wasn't sure about her at all.

'Any more questions?' she snapped.

'Yes. Several.'

'Well, get them off your chest, then perhaps I can get dressed.'

'Who told you that I had gone to Spain?'

'Max,' Sue replied. 'I have already told you.'

'And the telephone call that brought you to my hotel the other evening?'

Sue sighed. 'There was a message left for me. I don't know who had left it.'

'Don't you?' Stack asked.

'No, damn you, I don't.'

'The other night, you were going to tell me something.'

'I was going to tell you that for the past two days I have been followed wherever I have gone and I don't like it.'

'Then why didn't you telephone the police?'

'I did!'

Stack was taken aback. If Sue had telephoned the police, then it put her in a different light.

'Who did you speak to?' he said.

'Eventually, Lieutenant Keller. Before that I don't know.'

'What did he say?'

'That he would look into it.'

Either Sue was a damned good liar, or she was telling the truth. She had never been a liar before, he thought.

She looked at him, pleadingly.

'For goodness' sake, John, what is going on?' she asked. 'I've been worried sick about you. When you didn't turn up at the hotel the other night, I didn't know what had happened to you.'

'That's a change,' Stack said.

'Is it?' she asked. 'Perhaps you never noticed before.'

He shrugged. There had been faults on both sides. He was beginning to regret it. She looked so damned appealing.

'When did Ruddi decide to go to Bonn?' he asked.

'Yesterday.'

'You go to the studio?'

'No. Ruddi told me after the show, the other night, that he wouldn't need me for a couple of days or so.'

About the time Lehna had vanished from the airport, Stack thought.

198

'Were you surprised?' he asked.

'Yes, very. We hadn't finished the Harper contract.'

Stack grunted. It wasn't like Ruddi to cut short the Harper contract. It was a big, juicy contract that was going to set the advertising world alight, and make Ruddi internationally known. What else had tempted him away, Stack wondered?

'Does the name Fraulein Rosier mean anything to you?' he asked.

'She your friend?'

'How did you know?'

'Ruddi told me.'

Ruddi knows a hell of a lot, Stack thought. A hell of a lot.'

'See her at the studio?'

Sue shook her head.

'What about Franz Hessler?'

'He was one of the men in the processing department,' Sue replied.

That was true enough, Stack thought.

'He was accidentally killed in a car crash,' Sue added.

'Accidentally?' Stack asked suspiciously.

'So I was told,' Sue replied.

Perhaps Sue was still innocent, he thought. He looked at her hard and long. She was telling the truth, he thought. You don't have to live with a person for very long without getting to know when they are telling the truth or lying.

Sue looked at him, defiantly, as if she realised what he was thinking.

'I don't know what has got into you,' she snapped, 'but I don't like your manner. I'm beginning to wish I had let them keep you in the Eastern Zone.'

'Let them?' Stack asked suspiciously. 'There was a choice?'

'So I was told.'

Stack frowned. Schmidt had been cashing in all round, he thought.

'How much did they get out of you?' he asked.

'Two thousand marks,' Sue replied, 'for initial expenses. The rest later.'

'Forget the rest,' Stack said.

'I'm beginning to doubt whether you were even worth the down payment,' Sue said dryly.

Stack ignored the remark. He was thinking of Schmidt. Schmidt was a rotten, scheming mercenary, and he had been playing for time. Sue didn't know anything. She was innocent. But not Ruddi, he thought. Ruddi was in it somewhere. Ruddi bothered him, especially after what Sue had told him about the Harper contract. He decided to go to Ruddi's studio. It wasn't like Ruddi to cut short a fat contract without a good reason. And there was the link with Hessler.

'Where's your car?' he asked. 'I would like to borrow it.'

'In the garage,' she replied. 'Will you be back?'

'I'll return the car,' he replied gruffly.

'I wasn't meaning that,' she persisted.

Stack looked up at her.

'Perhaps,' he said evasively.

'I hope so,' she said as he left her.

Stack drove fast. Sue's car was a Mercedes sports which responded to the delicate touch of the accelerator. Lieffer's men had a difficult job to keep up with him. In Kaiser Friedrich Strasse Stack lost them and finished the journey solo.

The studio was a converted warehouse on the banks of the canal. The entrance was in a side lane. So was the rear exit. Stack parked his car and made for the rear exit. There were several other cars parked about, but none that he recognised.

The lock on the small rear door turned and the door opened. Stack, stealthily, stepped into the cool, dark atmosphere of the studio. He had a vague idea of the layout. There were a series of small cubicles surrounding a central stage. Overhead, a balcony of offices ran the full width of the building, and over the floor would be lengths of cables leading to the numerous light fittings. Stack remained quite still. The place had a feel about it of being unoccupied. He had backed a loser, he thought, but he decided to take a look in Ruddi's office, just in case. There was a link somewhere, he thought.

Carefully he picked his way over the loose cables and made for the corner staircase. As he reached the central stage area, two thoughts flashed simultaneously through his mind. Firstly – if the place was deserted, why had no one locked the rear exit door? And, secondly – he should have skirted the wall and not tried to take a short cut. But it was too late. As the thoughts entered his mind, he was suddenly held in the brilliant light from a barrage of arc lamps. The area had in a flash become transformed into an Aladdin's cave.

'Don't move,' a voice shouted, 'or you will be shot!'

A revolver spat fire, and a bullet passed perilously close to Stack's head. He stood quite still. He recognised the voice – it was Schmidt's!

'That's just a warning,' Schmidt called out.

'Schmidt?' Stack called back. He got no answer.

Frantically he looked at the floodlights. They surrounded him. He was a lonely figure on the stage.

'We meet again, Herr Stack,' Schmidt called to him, and laughed.

The man was twisted, Stack thought desperately.

'You are an actor on the stage,' Schmidt yelled, and fired twice.

The bullets smacked into the floor close to Stack's feet. Stack jumped to one side, towards one of the lamps. Schmidt laughed again.

'How much will you pay me now?' Schmidt called out.

'Where is Fraulein Rosier?' Stack yelled back, and moved about the stage. It was important to keep moving, he thought. He had to present Schmidt with a difficult target. The revolver wasn't the ideal weapon for accuracy. Unless Schmidt was an expert.

'I have her here,' Schmidt laughed.

'Then why can't we do a deal?' Stack yelled to him.

'Because I have already made a deal,' Schmidt called out. 'Stand still!' He fired again. The bullet tore into the floor close to where Stack was standing. He was an expert, Stack thought grimly, and cursed. He stood still. The perspiration started to roll down his brow from the heat of the lamps.

'I expected you coming here,' Schmidt called out, 'but I needed time to make my deal.' He started to laugh. 'You want to know what it is?'

Stack had a shrewd idea, but he also needed time.

'Yes,' he shouted. 'You tell me.'

'You die!' Schmidt laughed. 'You die and we get paid for it. That's what I call good business, because you had to die in any case. You tricked us, Stack.'

Stack swallowed hard.

'Don't be a fool, Schmidt,' he called back to him. 'Do you think I have come alone? The place is surrounded. Lieutenant Keller's men have come with me.'

'You lie!'

There was a sound of desperation in Schmidt's voice. He wasn't going to be held off much longer, Stack thought.

Bang! Suddenly a lamp bulb exploded. The noise made Stack jump. His brain immediately told him to take advantage of it. Schmidt would also have been taken off guard. There was a sudden area of darkness. Stack moved like lightning. He flung himself into the darkness, crashing into the fittings. Two bullets smacked into the floor close to his body. But Schmidt had been that fraction too late.

Stack picked himself up as an arc lamp was being turned in his direction. He brought out his revolver and fired two quick shots at the lamp. The light went out. Stack moved away before Schmidt returned the fire.

A grey light from the rear door attracted Stack's attention. Some reinforcements had arrived, he thought. Were they his or Schmidt's?

Schmidt fired at the open door. The door

immediately closed. Stack fired at the flash from Schmidt's revolver. There was a groan. Schmidt had been hit.

Crack! Crack! Two more shots were fired. They took Stack by surprise. They hadn't come from Stack or Schmidt. Stack looked up at the balcony and saw Schmidt's body delicately balanced on the guard rail. It swayed on the rail, as if uncertain which way to fall. Finally it moved forward and dropped with a thump on to the stage. Schmidt was dead.

'John!'

It was Lehna.

'Lehna!' Stack replied. 'Are you all right?'

'Yes.'

Stack turned the lamps around to illuminate the area. He saw Lehna on the balcony, as the rear door again opened and Lieutenant Keller burst into the studio with his men.

'Oh, John,' Lehna called out.

Stack went to meet her. She came down the iron staircase and rushed into his arms. As he held her to him, he saw Hendrich Lieffer standing over Schmidt's body. Lieutenant Keller came up to Stack.

'Where do we talk?' he asked. 'Here, or at my office?'

'Here,' Stack replied.

It was a room about three metres square

where they took Lehna. The walls were painted to depict various seasons of the year. Lehna sat on a seat in front of a summer beach scene. Her hair was dishevelled, but she was recovering from her shock. Her timely intervention had put paid to Schmidt and helped Stack. He was grateful.

Lieffer stood in the doorway. He made a fractional movement of his hand, indicating that he would like to speak to Stack and Lieutenant Keller. The two men joined him outside the room. Together they walked slowly around the stage.

'Was Schmidt one of yours?' Stack asked, indicating the body lying motionless on the floor with a cover over it.

'He was one of my senior deputies at the Ministry,' Lieffer replied calmly. 'He worked in my records department. An efficient man, but obviously greedy.'

'You suspected him?'

'And everyone,' Lieffer replied, and stood still. The two other men also stood quite still. Lieffer looked at Stack. 'Including Fraulein Rosier,' he added quietly. They exchanged glances. 'I received this from Major Roberts a few minutes ago,' he said, and handed Stack a decoded message.

Stack glanced at it. It was the answers to some of the queries he had sent to his Control. They were very much as he had suspected.

'How much authority have you?' he asked.

'Enough,' Lieffer replied.

Stack grunted.

'Let me speak to her alone,' he asked.

Again the two men looked into each other's eyes.

'You're wasting your time,' Lieffer remarked quietly.

'I would still like to try,' Stack persisted.

Lieffer withdrew a cigar case.

'I like a few minutes' smoke now and then,' he said vaguely. 'I'll give you five minutes, Herr Stack.'

'Thanks.'

Stack went back to the studio. Lehna looked up at him and smiled. Lieutenant Keller spoke to the other detectives in the room, and they left Stack alone with Lehna. Stack closed the door and took a seat facing Lehna.

'We know that the man they tried to get out of East Germany was not Criller,' he said convincingly. 'We know who he was and why he was being sent to Berlin.'

Lehna brushed her hair to one side and looked at him.

'If you will co-operate,' Stack added, 'I can arrange for you to be quietly smuggled back East.'

The look on Lehna's face changed fractionally.

'What do you mean?' she asked.

Stack repeated his offer.

'I don't know what you are talking about,' Lehna persisted.

Stack sighed. She was going to prove difficult.

'Let me spell it out more plainly,' he said. 'We know that you are a Communist agent. We know that you were part of a plot to bring an assassin into Berlin. We know that you used Lorenzo to suit your own ends. That you used me.'

'You are insane,' Lehna gasped. 'That is a pack of lies.'

'No, Lehna,' Stack said patiently. 'We have checked up on you. We know that Lehna Rosier does not now live in Israel. We know that she is in the United States.' He looked pleadingly into her eyes. 'Don't you see – we know!'

She dropped her eyes. For several seconds nothing was said.

'And how long have you suspected this?' she asked quietly.

'I suppose from the moment Henri Gallon was murdered,' Stack replied. 'It couldn't have been because of what he would have found out about me, or Lorenzo. Lorenzo has been in Barcelona for many a year. It had to be because of you.'

She said nothing.

'And your timely disappearance here in Berlin,' Stack went on. 'You knew it would take a little while for our Intelligence to run the rule over you. You thought that by the time they got their answers it would be too late for them to do anything. By then I would have been taken into the East and you would be out of circulation. Oh, I know I went voluntarily into East Berlin, but if I had not, I would have been taken there forcibly. You must have paid a lot of money to Schmidt's organisation to get such good service.'

Lehna still remained silent.

'Your sudden appearance in Barcelona was also a little too timely,' Stack added. 'Your people wanted someone close to me all the time. It so happens that I had lost my memory. What would you have done if I hadn't?'

She looked up at him.

'It would have been the same,' she said quietly.

'And killing Schmidt was a last-ditch effort to turn things in your favour?' Stack asked.

'He was a sewer rat,' Lehna replied. 'He deserved no pity.' She smiled faintly. 'Perhaps I did it to save you,' she added, smiling. 'I will tell them that.'

'You do,' Stack said, but he knew that wasn't the real reason why she had done it.

'Who gave you your orders in Berlin?' he asked.

She shook her head.

'No deal,' she said quietly.

'But you will go to prison,' Stack persisted.

'And I will eventually be released,' she said. 'I am quite young. They will not forget me. They also have their code of honour. They will do an exchange. They aren't really monsters.'

He looked into her eyes. She looked as she always had – young and helpless. He knew that she was otherwise, but he preferred to think of her like that.

'It could be a long time,' he said. 'If you help…'

She shook her head.

'You are too late,' she intervened, and looked away.

Too late! What did she mean? Too late for what?

'For what?' he asked.

She looked at him and he saw another side to her. The side that had made her a Communist agent. She was mocking him. He swung around on his heels and left the studio. Lieffer and Lieutenant Keller looked at him anxiously.

'No dice,' Stack said.

'Then let us take a ride and talk about it,' Lieffer said calmly. 'Come.'

He quickly led Stack out of the warehouse to where a convoy of large, sleek, black, official-looking cars was waiting to move off. Alongside the cars stood a row of Federal Intelligence agents. Lieffer took Stack to one of the cars. Inside was a small television screen and two-way radio equipment which kept Lieffer informed of the progress of the state visit. On the screen was a picture of the West German Chancellor and Yugoslav President, at the airport.

'They'll be at the Senate in Schoneberg in an hour,' Lieffer said seriously.

Stack sat back in the upholstered seat. Lieffer sat beside him, grim but calm. It reflected the atmosphere of the city. The sun was shining, but the brightness and colour was only on the surface. There was also uncertainty and anticipation in the air.

'She said we were too late,' Stack said quietly.

The car glided silently away from its parking space.

'Too late for what?' Lieffer asked. 'The assassination?'

'I don't know,' Stack said, frowning, 'but that was my impression.'

'Too late,' Lieffer said quietly to himself. 'Too late.' He turned to Stack. 'We have every vantage point covered. The official party will be in a bullet-proof car. How else could he be assassinated?'

'A bomb?' Stack asked thoughtfully.

Lieffer considered the problem.

'It could be,' he said. 'It could be.'

He picked up the radio microphone and crisply issued a series of orders that would send an army of men into all the rooms that were to be used by the official guest. When he had finished giving his orders, he sat back alongside Stack. But he wasn't relieved. Stack could feel his tension.

'You have had Fraulein Rosier followed since her arrival in Berlin?' Stack asked.

'Yes, but she gave us the slip at the airport when she went to ground.'

'She visited Franz Hessler on Sunday evening.'

'Agreed.'

'Who was Hessler?'

'The genuine link between the Rosier family and the Crillers in Leipzig,' Leiffer said. 'He used to work for a film manufacturing company. About two months ago, he joined Ruddi's studio.'

'And his death?'

'More than likely engineered. He had to be got rid of before Fraulein Rosier arrived or he would have realised the whole business with Criller was a fabrication.'

'And the real Criller?'

'Probably under lock and key somewhere in East Germany.'

'They had it all planned out very carefully,' Stack said pensively.

There was an impatient buzz on the radio

telephone. Lieffer took the call. He acknowledged the message and replaced the receiver.

'We picked up Ruddi Schoner about half an hour ago,' he said. 'He isn't talking – yet.'

'They are all keeping tight-lipped,' Stack said. It made him feel even more certain that something was planned.

'Ruddi was involved,' Lieffer said grimly. 'We'll get him to talk eventually.'

Eventually would be too late, Stack thought.

They turned on to the ring road and headed towards Schoneberg. The leading car blasted its siren to give the convoy right of way. On the television screen, the Yugoslav President and the German Chancellor could be seen leaving the guard of honour.

'They'll be at the Town Hall in a few minutes,' Lieffer said, tight lipped.

Stack stared blankly out of the window. It had all been carefully planned, he thought. Everything neatly worked out. They had known about Gunter just as they had known about Berak. They had wanted to find out what Gunter had got wind of. What he was going to pass on to Stack. They knew of the link. Gunter had been sent to Spain. Preiser and his agents had gone to keep watch on him. It was one of Preiser's men that had attacked Stack in the mountains. Stack had fought him off. The man must have then followed Stack in his car and ran off the road. He hadn't been dead when Stack had left him. Stack remembered now. He moved impatiently in his seat. They knew he would go to Spain, he thought. They had it planned for Lorenzo to contact him. They knew he would be sent to Spain...

The convoy turned off the ring road. Lieffer took a call over his radio and issued a further series of orders.

They knew that he was going to Spain, Stack thought. Just as they had known that Gunter would be sent there. They had also known that Stack was in East Berlin when he had gone in search of Criller. He grunted audibly. Lieffer looked at him, but Stack was far away. He was thinking of the other doubts that at times had troubled him. Berak hadn't had the same success in Berlin that he had managed in Prague. There had been the failures, and his suspicions. The opposition had got on to him too quickly for Stack's liking. And Gunter also. They had thought that the leak had been through one of Berak's contacts, but had that been the whole story? Had it not also been through Stack himself? Had they not also flushed him? He had kept himself in a very strict, disciplined routine, he thought. No one had been allowed to get close to him. No one. That had been his weakness. Or had it? Had it not also been his strength? No one had been allowed to get close to him. No one other than... Again he grunted audibly. They had also brought Sue into the game. Lehna had showed him Sue's picture to throw him, and keep him interested. They had kept Sue in reserve at Ruddi's studio so that they could use her as additional bait. They had known all about her, just as they had known that Schmidt had worked for Lieffer. That Schmidt had access to Lieffer's records. So it was around the same circle again, he thought. Always pointing to the same person. But how were they going to carry out their assassination? How? How?

They came to the John F Kennedy Platz and the Schoneberg Town Hall. The atmosphere was charged and noisy. The square was crowded with spectators and demonstrators. A line of white-helmeted police kept them away from the receiving bay. As Lieffer's convoy came to a halt, the Liberty Bell from the Town Hall tower started tolling. It was immediately joined by a noisy barrage of anti-Yugoslav slogans and fireworks, until the demonstrators realised that the tolling bell only indicated the time and was not greeting the official party. The noise from the demonstrators subsided, but a clash between one of the groups and the police continued.

Stack saw it all at a glance and felt the acute, electric tension. He also saw the official welcoming party at the foot of the steps, surrounded by police and Press photographers. And he saw Max Schafer. It wasn't difficult to pick him out. He was wearing his colourful bow tie and had the inevitable cigar in his mouth. He stood behind the other Press men at the top of the steps. There was a camera with large telescopic lens slung around his neck.

Stack looked hard at him. It was always Max Schafer that Stack's suspicions turned to. Everything pointed to Schafer. Everything.

'He didn't even know Lorenzo,' Stack muttered, as if trying to finalise his thoughts.

'Who didn't?' Lieffer asked sharply.

'Max,' Stack replied.

'That's surprising,' Lieffer said. 'I thought Max would...'

Stack heard no more. He saw Max touch the camera hanging from his neck, and the camera seemed to magnify in size. Stack felt his throat go dry and his pulse start to take off. He recalled what Sue had told him about Ruddi. Ruddi used to be an instrument maker, she had said. My God! Stack thought. That does it. It had to be the camera!

'The camera!' Stack exploded. 'We've got to stop him.'

'Who?' Lieffer shouted, and held Stack back.

'Max,' Stack called out. 'That camera is loaded!'

Stack got out of the car as the official party drove into the square. He didn't hear Lieffer shouting his orders. He didn't hear the fireworks, the yelling, the shouting, the cheering, the scuffling. Nor did he see the clash between the demonstrators and the police, or the official welcoming party move to greet the two Heads of State. All he saw was the straight-laced cigar-smoking Max Schafer, standing by himself at the top of the steps – and the camera.

Stack ran as fast as he could. Hot on his heels were two Federal men. A figure appeared in front of Stack. He side-stepped it and reached the steps. He saw Schafer take hold of his camera.

'No, Max!' Stack yelled. 'No!'

He ran up the steps and collided with Schafer as he was taking aim. Two other bodies also flung themselves on to the man.

Schafer collapsed to the ground under the barrage of flesh and muscles. More of Lieffer's men gathered around. The pomp of the state visit continued unperturbed. The visiting party stepped out of the cars. The crowds cheered, or demonstrated, according to their allegiance. The scuffle with Schafer was lost in the heat of the emotions and aura of the occasion. Schafer was bodily lifted from the ground and taken to the Town Hall.

Stack watched. There was a slight hold up at the entrance to the building. Schafer turned and looked at Stack. Their eyes met. There was no look of sadness in Schafer's eyes – no look of friendship – no look of animosity – no look of anything. It was just a blank. Stack felt sorry. He had hoped for some indication to show that their friendship had meant something, but there was no such sign. Schafer looked away and was man-handled into the building.

Ah! What the hell? Stack thought. Why should he worry? He thought of Berak instead and felt better. Perhaps Berak would have forgiven him if he had known, he thought, and Gunter also. Perhaps he could now forgive himself. He walked slowly back across the square to Lieffer's car, and stood leaning against its polished bodywork. The sun felt warm on his face. It was all over, he thought. It was finished, and so was he. They couldn't use him again for some time. He had been too exposed. He felt as if a weight had been removed from his shoulders. As if his inside was starting to thaw. He turned his back on the car and watched Lieffer walking towards him.

'You were right about the camera,' Lieffer said quietly as he came up to Stack. 'Thanks – John.'

Stack looked at him and smiled. 'That's okay,' he said.

'Would he have used it?' Lieffer asked.

Stack shrugged. You have to be married to something or somebody, he thought. Max Schafer had said that, and with Max it hadn't been the Press business, or a wife. Max Schafer had been married to their cause. The look on his face had told Stack that.

'If it was loaded, he would have used it,' Stack said, and forgot about Max Schafer.

'What now?' Lieffer asked cheerfully.

What now, Stack wondered? What was going to fill the vacuum now? Before he had got involved, it had been Sue. She had occupied all his time. Sue! The very thought of her made him feel a warm glow inside.

'I think I will go and invite my wife out to lunch,' he said enthusiastically.

Lieffer smiled. 'Good,' he said warmly. 'I'm pleased, because she's waiting for you.' He moved his head to indicate the end of the convoy of cars. 'I brought her along just in case.'

'You did!' Stack exclaimed. 'You did!' He looked along the line of cars and saw Sue. She waved and smiled at him.

'Sue!' he called out, his excitement increasing. 'Sue!' They ran towards each other and met halfway. He took her in his arms and held her close. The iceberg inside of him had all melted. His winter was over.

The publishers hope that this book has given you enjoyable reading. Large Print Books are especially designed to be as easy to see and hold as possible. If you wish a complete list of our books please ask at your local library or write directly to:

Magna Large Print Books
Magna House, Long Preston,
Skipton, North Yorkshire.
BD23 4ND

This Large Print Book, for people
who cannot read normal print,
is published under the auspices of

THE ULVERSCROFT FOUNDATION